K.J. SCHMUTZ

JUSTIN'S QUEST

EARTH HOLIDAY

20 Twenty Literary Group

Justin's Quest

ISBN
978-1-961250-29-1 (Paperback)
978-1-961250-30-7 (eBook)

Justin's Quest:
Earth Holiday

by

K. J. Schmutz

TABLE OF CONTENTS

Introduction vii
Prologue 1

Chapter 1 Hull 3
Chapter 2 Mars 4
Chapter 3 Homeward Bound 19
Chapter 4 Telling the Others 32
Chapter 5 After School 42
Chapter 6 Adventure...Maybe 56
Chapter 7 Drawn by Light 64
Chapter 8 Where Are We? 69
Chapter 9 Ghost Ship...The Manix IV 73
Chapter 10 Life Rush 76
Chapter 11 Change of Plans, and Time Door 82
Chapter 12 Cause and effect 88
Chapter 13 Piloting A Ship Within A Ship 97
Chapter 14 178 Light-Years Away 110
Chapter 15 Who Invited You 115
Chapter 16 Life Rush Second 118
Chapter 17 Bad Outcome 124
Chapter 18 More reasons to Act 126
Chapter 19 Unit's forty-two gift 129
Chapter 20 Permission to Board the Felix One 132
Chapter 21 Advancing the Plan 137
Chapter 22 Decks and Suits 142
Chapter 23 The M.T.T. and Dagger in the Back 146
Chapter 24 The Daggers Twist 148
Chapter 25 Now or Never 151
Chapter 26 Too Little to Late 154
Chapter 27 Captured 157

INTRODUCTION

Three Large alien ships of green and gold, four thick disks linked together in the middle with large tubes that created a circular design. There were lights that moved across the tubes as it moved closer and closer to approach Earth's defenses platforms. The defenses group had recognized them as the Gillenium battle carriers. The defense platforms that were stationed high above the surface drilled in preparing for the possibility of combat.

Far below the defense platforms laid Earth, currently in a frozen dead state, but it is still a critical asset and symbol to mankind. Time was of the essence to ready itself to fight off the now approaching alien threat.

"Several ships on long range scanners, they appear to be on an intercept course with Earth."

"Prepare to raise shields"

"All systems are online."

"Communication channels are open, and broadcasting on all frequencies. No response, they do not appear to be backing down. We will have to defend ourselves."

The orbital space stations used their boosters to come together to block the incoming ships.

"Shields up."

The four stations came together and a bluish transparent energy shield covered an area between the stations. Multiple small fighters were launched from the station and engaged the enemy. Of the fighters, weapon platform ships we diverted from lunar customs to aid protection of the Earth, the weapon platform were larger than a three-story building, with crews of fifty or sixty people targeting the Gillenium threat.

"The three ships are not stopping. They're going to hit the shields!"

Upon impact, the smaller fighters blasted away at one of the large ships drawing away the lead ship, which backed off. There was an explosion. After the smoke had cleared and the bright glow had dissipated, one of the stations was gone.

"Sir, station Delta 451, it's… it's gone."

"Search for remains, and report back to me."

"Yes, Sir."

"Sir, there is no Debris from the Delta 451 station, but there are odd remains of a subspace opening, and we only found debris from two of the alien threats. My conclusion is that two of the ships were decoys and one of the ships was trying to capture one of our stations."

"But why?"

"Unknown, Sir. Moving back to ready position."

"Understood, carry on."

Many of the warring worlds who fought over control of the universe set aside their upheaval to come together to form the Gillenium Council in order to obtain a new discovery in technology called the Matter Transportation Transmitter (M.T.T.) created by the Canero race. The Canero people refused to share the technology because of its power and potential to be abused, because the M.T.T. did much more than move an object from one location to another. Hunted now by a newly formed Gillenium Council across the length and breadth of space for this technology, the race was driven to extinction. Because the Canero people knew the Gillenium Council would use the technology to enslave the universe. The Canero people used their power to prevent the Gillenium Council from obtaining the M.T.T. When the M.T.T. was created the scientists used a fragment of time, thus the M.T.T. became a part of time, always existing from the beginning of time to the end of time. The only means to truly defeat the creation of the Gillenium Council, to prevent the extinction of the Canero race, and all the other repercussions across the universe is to destroy the M.T.T. even in present time, but such a powerful device, could you make that decision? Would you use it for your own personal gain, or the right choice? Will you be destroyed by your own selfish greed if misused?

Final thoughts: Wishing that you and others make great decision, for they have both positive and negative impacts, "All things are a matter of time"

K. J. Schmutz

PROLOGUE

"Humans!" Lord Nac Wer shouted from inside his small one man listening post station as he was monitoring activity near the Crab Nebula.

Lord Nac Wer, who stood an amazing eleven feet tall, though still a few feet shorter than Sir Yid, and certainly a few planets short of a solar system. Lord Wer was on punishment detail, which means watching the monitoring feed from Gillenium controlled space, and the surrounding sectors. It was boring, annoying, and not monitoring avoidances meant certain death. As each sensor feed contacted the listening post, Lord Nac Wer entered the sensors number, researched their activities, and made sure to follow step by step the explicit rules, making detailed reports of what happens during the monitoring, sending it up for authorization, then on to the next feed.

"It looks like they're heading back to Mars, from Planet Wells," He couldn't believe he was even bothered by the thought of the insignificant little pests.

Before Lord Nac Wer could switch to another monitoring feed, the scanner displayed the ship; a flashing image came across his screen. Lord Nac Wer angrily shouted. "That's a subspace signal, it's coming from the Human craft, but humans don't have subspace technologies.

Now amazed, his face lit up excitedly as he thought, "Wait, humans don't have subspace technologies!"

His eyes grew wide. "They must have found something on Wells! I know it; I can't let humans have the Wells tech. That ship

That ship is called the Solid Luck. Funny, after I am through with them, they won't feel so lucky."

Lord Wer continued doing his calculations. "That ship will reach Mars in about four more rotations and twenty rills. I will have to act fast; the Hassar will cut it close. It will be there in only four rotations and seventeen rills. Sir Yid will be happy when I give him the news!" Lord Nac Wer said, laughing to himself, as he finalized the orders to destroy the small transport.

CHAPTER ONE

HULL

A massive hull materialized as it passed through a barrier of subspace and below a medium sized planet of blue and green, bombarded by comets, rocks and other objects from the heavens. As the craft studied the planet closely, a large asteroid struck the craft. The asteroid bounced off the hull of the ship projecting it into space, while the craft lost control rapidly plunged uncontrollably toward the planet surface. The craft crashed, creating a chain reaction, changing all life presently on the planet surface. Afterwards the remains of the alien craft slowly sank and embedded itself in the planet's center.

For countless eons the alien ship from the stars has been held captive in the center of the planet known as Earth. As life grew on Earth, nature progressed, and the craft in the middle of the planet deteriorated over the course of four billion years, to which the planet became toxic from the contents of the eroding craft. Mankind was forced to move out into the stars and begin anew. Only a handful of planets such as Mars were deemed to be fit for colonization through terraforming. Many of the planets that were unsuitable to colonize were mined for needed material and other resources for the few inhabitable planets to continue providing their earth like conditions.

The year is 2709 A.D. Wednesday May 12th, Life for the human race is now slowly rebuilding.

CHAPTER TWO

MARS

The Solid Luck was returning to Mars after a routine maintenance and resource gathering operation on a five day mission to a mysterious planet known as Planet Wells.

On a large screen mounted to the wall, a planet came into view. The image grew larger and larger. “Mars,” a computerized voice boomed.

Two men stood looking at a screen on the wall and one reached out to touch the lower part of the screen, which then displayed a text that detailed the duties onboard the vessel. The vessel is the Solid Luck, a large scout vessel that was revamped into a small transport, mostly for traveling between Mars and planet Wells, with a crew of forty entirely made up of technicians. Wells was considered an out-of-place rouge planet caught in an elliptical orbit between our solar system and Alpha Centauris solar system, but had many Earth like resources. Wells also has a deadly secret, though not much larger than Earth, the gravity is forty-five times the earths, or fifty-two times the gravity of Mars, but what catches the eye, if you can see it, Wells is partially transparent, however, no one knows why, but there are many theories as to why.

“Next to my wife, that is the most beautiful view. But man, it is good to be going home. Those dang robots, always needing to be repaired… And Planet Wells’ gravity, it’s a killer for those machines," one man said to the other. "The gravity is pretty rough for them, it wears them out, and they are always going to need repairs, or parts replaced. Besides, why are you complaining? Do you want to go down there and mine yourself? That's suicide."

"OK, on second thought, no, so send a machine. I am not going down there. I never have, and I hope I never will. I am just glad that the orbital elevator can power above the planets field of gravity, orbit is as close as I am getting," the other man said agreeing that this was best.

"We will be touching down on Mars in approximately forty minutes, at the MMA at the north polar region. A transport will see you two gentlemen home," The computerized voice boomed again.

The two men turned to each other, both with a sigh of relief.

Steven Haysting who stood a whopping six-four and bright red hair, his artificial eye almost seemed natural except for the appearance of wires that budge out of the skin of his surrounding temple. He is the father of Justin, Chris, Curtis, and Sam. Is the senor most mechanic, and engineering genius to come out of the Martian Mining Association.

John Parson at an average five-eight stalky, bald on top with a long thick goatee that almost covers the data port connecter that draped over his shoulder connected to the back of his neck. He is the father of Nicole is an expert programmer for the Martian Mining Association, but because of the atmosphere of planet wells any software tweaking to the mining machines has to be done in close proximity of the planet's surface.

Both men wore a jumpsuit, thought looking at it, it was as a low resolution image had been casted over their bodies, these were holo-cloth suits, some of the users of holo-cloth could create more defined clothing, or moving objects in front or on the clothing but a great deal of conscious concentration was needed to keep the appearance in a viewable resolution and active.

"Man, these fourteen-hour days are killing me. I can't wait to get home and enjoy some of my wife's programming," Steven Haysting said.

"So Steve, I hear that your boy Justin has asked my daughter to prom at social school. Aren't you excited?" John Parson asked, after looking at his arm with a new incoming message that displayed above his skin.

"Excited? Well, why not? Those two have been dating for the last three years, and have both attended every social event at the Red Sands and every other social school they both have gone to," Steve said.

The rear door slid open to the room the two men were talking in, behind them as a stout cylinder table announced it entrances to the two gentlemen. "Good afternoon gentlemen. Care for some coffee to drink?" a soft electronic feminine voice asked as the small table entered into the room. Its appearance was of a circular wooden coffee table. The center of the table was a large round base that led to the floor, which sported a hover unit allowing it to move silently above the ground. "Coffee," both men said at the same time, and then laughed.

The sides of the table slid open, exposing metal cups, as an arm removed two and placed them on top. A nozzle rose above the cups, filling them with a thin black steamy substance.

"Yeah, and speaking of being invited, they went to a few events they weren't invited to!" John added, laughing.

"Would either of you gentlemen like cream or sugar?" the table asked. Both men answered 'no' as they reached for a cup and started to sip the steaming beverage. The table slipped out the same door through which it had entered moments ago.

A sudden jolt shook through the hull of the ship, the sound of twisting metal and shattering glass was heard from above the room the gentlemen shared. Both men looked towards the sound, and then turned to each other with worried expressions. A blast erupted once again from above as both men were thrown to the floor as the ship rocked to one side, their coffees spilling on their holo-clothes, the carpeted floor and wall near the screen. A second jolt was felt from above, followed by a terrible crash from below, throwing the two men around the room as though the ship was hitting the ground like a ton of bricks.

The Solid Luck, had rapidly descended through Mars now terraformed atmosphere, and struck the red soft soil, as it plowed at incredible speed towards the North Polar Region Martian Mining facility.

"What was that?" both said at the same time as they tried to roll over and lift themselves off the ground, now on their feet they both struggled to keep their balance feeling the ship was still moving across the rocky ground as the ship rocked back and forth and rattled. "I don't know, well find out" one answered.

The ship was kicking up large plumes of red dust. Panels on the underbelly of the ship and sides were ripped off as it scraped across the surface of the planet as momentum carried the Solid Luck straight towards the building.

Another crash over took the ship as it struck the side of the Martian Mining Facility, the thirteen ton vessel made an eerie sound as the hull bucked under it weight, before settling, and then a deafening silence. The interior lighting went out as the power failed. John could see Steven artificial eye glowing in the dark room. The dim emergency lighting flickered on, establishing that the two men were thrown on their backs as smoke trickled into the room from above.

The Solid Luck struck the side of the Martian Mining facility. The Martin Mining Facility, a large twelve story building, covered in sheets of glass. The inverted shape of the building is as if someone stuck an upside down pyramid in the middle of the crimson sands. The Facility is responsible for finding resources that Mars lacks to sustain and preserve comfortable living conditions so life and families can prosper on the once barren planet.

Where the large refitted scout craft struck was about ten yards away from landing pad five. As blinding flashes of light flickered and sparks sputtered from the metal and glass structure, smoke billowed from both the craft and building, as fire shot out of the building licking the side of the remains of the Solid Luck.

A crewman rushed into the screen room. "Steve, John, you two all right? We just struck the side of our drop off point" the crewman shouted.

"You mean where we were going to drop off all the ore we collected from Wells?" John asked.

"The very same, are you two ok to walk?" The crewman asked.

"Yeah, I am fine, but someone owes me a coffee," Steven pointed depressingly to an empty coffee tin. "I am good," John remarked. "Steven let's worry about the coffee later" John finished. "Quickly, We need to get out of here!" the crewman exclaimed. "Is everyone else okay?" John asked. "No time. We must get you out of here. They will explain later, so quickly we must get out of here!" the crewmen yelled with excitement as he pelted down the hall he entered through.

As the three rushed from the room where once the duty rooster was displayed, they ran through the halls as they were beginning crumbling to the floor below them, one or two crewmen were buried in debris along the floor, and an arm was stretched out threw a blocked doorway along their path. One could see that through the cracks in the bulkhead that the damage was extensive. Too many of the small connecting halls and rooms were crushed with no way in or out. The three hurried trying to dodge wires and large sheets of metal hanging from the ceiling, as explosive sparks flickered from open panels that littered their perilous path to escape.

The three proceeded non-stop as fast as they could until they entered one of the many cargo holds the ship had to offer to store the ore that was collected, there several members of the crew were removing panels from the walls;

The three could see out of the open wall that it was a Martin night, but large lights on the side of the building illuminated the side of the ship, the crew was attempting to escape from.

Many of the other crew were were setting up portable airbags to throw below the cargo hull to offer escapers a softer landing for the injured that couldn't make the jump in the low gravity.

As the dust settled, the outlines of the crew could be seen as they escaped from the wreckage; the wounded were being carried by able crewmen. After the three exited the ship they noticed the remains of a smaller vessel sitting atop of the light transport through the spotlights pointing at the Solid Luck.

"It was the Hassar, look!, there's their ship," Steve stated pointing, they could seeing a number of small silvery figures exiting from the small craft or standing nearby it, now jumping off the top of the transport with no hesitation.

Sirens blared, and now all exterior lights from the building were fixated on the wreckage, as an announcer over a loud speaker gave direction to emergency personal that wounded were going to be in need of treatment out in front of the wreckage, unknown to them that there was still a threat of attackers present.

Emergency units rushed with spot lights on from the Martian transportation facility to treat the survivors, and extinguish the flames jetting from the wreckage not able to yet see the invaders still in the cover of darkness.

Reaching the Solid Luck the emergency personal exited their vehicles to begin treated the injured, and tackled the flaming inferno that once was a transport vessel. Some of the crews were ambushed by one of the fifteen small shiny skeletons like machines with spikes, claws, and one red lens that's fixed to the middle of its skull like head. The small machines flung themselves towards those uninjured and injured alike, slashing, and striking without fear or remorse. These were the Hassar Assassins models.

The Hassar: Though not much from a human perspective is known about this cyborg-like race of programed assassins. The human race first encountered the fierce weapons when debris entered our solar system with large alien words that later translated into "Beware the Hassar", and attacked those that examined the floating remains. We as humans have had deadly encounters many times after with this suicidal race, and if there are any chances of their task not being accomplished, they explode, hoping to cause as much collateral damage, which often has a devastating effect.

Now in the middle of a brutal ground attack, the few who manage to scurry undetected to the protection of the intact part of the Martian Mining Facility got away, or escaped into the night, others were not so lucky and got caught in the crossfire between the emergence response teams and the Hassar.

Five men rushed out of the nearby building dawning body armor, and laser emitters held in their palms sending a dazzling display of destruction toward the menacing threat that lit up when striking the mechanical menace.

Two Hassar machines jumped through the air to attack both John and Steve as they attempted to reach the safety of the facility. Multiple well placed energy beams hit the alien robots, though mostly immobilized, they were still lying on top of their targets attacking them. John managed to conjure a holo-cloth exoskeleton which was not strong enough for the high gravity of Jupiter or planet Wells, but was able to push off the Hassar on top of him, the suit appeared to be blurry, with jagged edges and pixelated imagery. John swung with a fist at the machine hard enough in the low Martian gravity that it landed hard against the pile of wreckage several feet away, making the assassin detonate. The shockwave of the explosion knocked over two members from the medical staff that were attempting to rescue another one of the victims who were lying on the ground near the Solid Luck, once back on their feet were able to drag the injured back to the building.

Steve was struggling with the machine that landed on him taking several swings, as he continued to roll around. Now standing upright, John quickly approached Steve to pull the assassin off of his injuries and held the machine in the air by the back of the spine.

"You want to mess with us? You picked the wrong tired, sore robotic repair personnel to mess with, and your toast bone-boy!" he said.

Of course the Hassar didn't speak English, and even if they did, they would have had to read John's lips, because the exoskeleton he was wearing prevented anyone from hearing him, unless they had accessed his COMM-channel.

John stared into the Hassar assassin's face. The Hassar tried to swipe at John, but John flung the droid behind his back, and then whipped his arm forward. He put his body weight into it he leaned forward and threw the robot towards the now-torched ship's rubble, which then exploded, collapsing a few panels, sending them towards the red sands causing a sudden plume of dust to rise.

John now looking down at Steven he mouthed some words, forgetting to remove his exoskeleton. "What?" said Steve asked, still lying on the ground? John's suit faded to a bright light and morphed back into the dark gray maintenance jumpsuit.

"I said, 'Whoa that was just to close, but who where they after?' I don't like this, and I think we should prepare for a second round of attacks.," John said now looking at Steven's wounds.

A crewmember came towards the two asking, "Are you alright?" "No, Steven is injured, get a medic team" John said.

The crewmember tapped at his COMM link just below the top of his shoulder. "We need a stretcher; another one of the engineers has been injured. We're near landing pad five, with the remains of the Solid Luck."

The COMM: a small thin box that attached to the skin near the clavicle bone of the shoulder. The COMM doesn't need to be touched directly, because it can sense when a hand is placed over it, even though the thickest of holo-cloth or clothing. The COMM sends the sound vibrations to the ear cannel, for the wearer to hear, though the COMM could be used as a speaker. The COMM could also be used to transmit pictures and video picked up through the users eyes, and picks up the vibration from around the neck and transmit the sound. Through the use of the COMM can be used to record audio and video, and can in a few instances be used as a real-time language translator.

John had been able to think quickly and shield himself from attacks. Steve however had a few gashes on his face and many deep cuts on his chest.

Two of the medical crew from inside the compound rushed out with a thin hovering stretcher and bright light emitted from their shoulders as they searched for the wounded. As they approached they shined their lights on the two. "Are you alight?"

Steve looked at John "I think today is a bad day if we need to be asked twice if we are alight" John laughed nodding his head, then looked up towards the two.

"I am, He needs attention." John said as he pointed towards Steve. The two carefully approached Steve, lifting him up, and slid the stretcher underneath him; once he was secure onboard the unit lifted up about waist level and cautiously proceeded to glide back into the emergency vehicle near the compound.

John stood up, and saw what was left of a metal skeleton lying on the ground, walked over and crouched over the remains of one of the Hassar that attacked. "There is one of the Hassar here, I need you to send out a tech team to take the remains of this machine, have its data bank analyzed, and see who the target of this attack was... Is everyone else alright?" John ordered over the COMM system.

"Yes Sir, I'll have someone retrieve the remains immediately, and everyone on the ground is accounted for, were going to have to send in a recovery team into the ship and search for survivors" A voice spoke back to John.

"Copy, I am going with Steven, we'll be in the medical facility, I need to speak with the one of directors from security."

"I'll send someone right away."

John hurried to catch up with medics as they rushed Steven inside.

John caught up to Steve who was being placed into the emergency vehicle heading to the Iron Dunes medical Unit close to the Martin Mining Facility. After arriving Steven was placed on a bed in the infirmary. John Meet up with one of the directors named Byron in an observation room next to the room where Steven waited for treatment. Byron who was over the Mining Facilities security talked with Steven about what information could be recovered. Moments later a tall young nurse entered into the treatment room, her yellow medical scrubs and an orange medical coat looked like a half pealed orange, she stood over him and pressed a few buttons on the side of the bed activating a holonull attached to the side of the bed as she introduced herself.

"I am nurse Sarah White, what seems to be the problem?" The nurse asked.

"We had a run in with these little fellows, they crashed our party." Steven responded.

The holonull beeped, then a high pitch sine was heard when it became active. Because of the holo-cloth projected his clothing, the medical facility had to removed Steven's ability to create holo-cloth to treat his injury, otherwise he could prevent the medical workers from treating his injuries by blocking the wounds by accidental projection of an article of clothing. Removing the projection of Steven's clothing exposing his body, the nurse could see his COMM box, which was damaged by the Hassar, and the other wounds just above the abdomen, and through the pectoral area.

"I can see that, and what happened here?"

"You removed my clothes."

"Ok, I resolve that first, then your wounds." Sarah said as she picked up a gown sheet, and reached over Steven's exposed torso, as her arms draped in her medical coat came closer to Steven's midsection, the sleeves of her coat disappeared. Draped the gown over Steven's torso area for modesty, she drew her arms back, as she did her sleeves reappeared. The nurse turned to her right side to pick up a package from a small tried that was held by an arm that extended from the ceiling. Opening the package to draw out a moist cloth, and approached Steven's face. The nurse cleaned his wounds on his face, as she did, the cuffs of her sleeves disappeared, only to return when she pulled her arms back, to deposit the soiled gauze onto a hazardous waist bin. Then the nurse turned back to the right and pulled second gauze from the wrapper to clean the deep gashes across his chest and upper abdomen. This special gauze from the package was infused with a probiotic fluid which would promote healing and prevent infection. After cleaning the multiple wounds across Steven's chest she placed the gauze on the metal tray now moved next to the bed Steven was laying on. The nurse picked up a handle with two thin flat rods on either side lying next to the gauze, this was a skin bonding hand-held device that grabbed micro layers of skin and bonded the molecules together, much like sutures but was more efficient in promoting natural healing, and took less time.

Steven noticed movement out of the corner of his eye, his attention was now turned to two figures that paced in the observation room.

"...I'm not sure how long, it's at the lab now." "And they will notify you if..." "Yes, even if they can't, I'll receive some word." John and Byron talked as they approached the glass in the adjoining observation room to see the nurse bent over Steven, as she finished the tissue bonding, the top of her coat and gown vanished showing a green scrub underneath, as well as seeing her coat sleeves and paints suit phase away, as she got closer to the area that the holonull effected. The two continued to watch through the glass panel.

"How is Steven?" Byron asked while placing his hand over his COMM which made communications between the two rooms possible.

"Well, he seemed to be progressing well. The tissue bonding will hold those wounds closed, and they will heal without leaving any scarring," the nurse stated, the two on lookers could hear the soft rumbling of the skin bonding hand-held device adjoined with the sine of the holonull.

Byron nodded his head as he did so he looked over at John, Who took a deep sigh of relief, knowing maybe soon if Justin and Nicole were to marry they would be family.

"Great! Well, what did I say? These fourteen-hour days are killing me. Say, did they ever find out who the Hassar were after?" Steve asked.

"Not yet, the Hassar remains are still being examined, but until then, I need to speak to both of you in private, when you feel up to it," Byron said.

"Was anyone killed?" asked Steve. "Unfortunately the captain was killed, as were a few crewmen that were on the upper levels near the Hassar craft, either by the crashing of the vessel or by getting in the way of the Hassar assassins," the director of security said sadly.

"You mean James? Damn those Hassar and their masters!" Steve said angrily.

"We did however find that the Hassar had an explosive on board their ship. That's why there was a huge explosion, thrusting the Solid Luck towards the ground like it did." the commanded said.

"Wish we could send the Gillenium Council an explosive or two," John said. "Oh right. Any human setting foot on that system is... well it's just suicide," Steve commented.

"What's with your unhealthy obsession with suicide, why do you think every risk is suicide?"

"Do not, I just fear for the worst."

"You said that about the mystery meal on the lunch menu was suicide when we left two days ago, you said that about mining on planet Wells is Suicide, what's with…"

"Ok enough, Steve will need his rest, why don't you and Byron come back later." The nurse stated. The two agreed and left the viewing room. The nurse turned back to Steven. "Comfortable?" "Just this pain in my knee from when I was returned, but other than that I am okay, thanks." Steven said as he remained laying. "Oh, you were one of those who were onboard the Delta 541, you were returned almost a year later." "I was." "What happened?" "I don't remember, it was like they wiped our memory before they returned us." The nurse walked to return the equipment and put a pitcher of water with a foam cup on a tray from a nearby table where the medical equipment was placed, and wheeled it over to the bed where Steven laid. "Nurse, could you please bring me a coffee, please, my coffee spilled." Steven smiled. "What coffee?" "It was on the Solid Luck, and we had some turbulence." The Nurse smiled and took the pitcher of water, as she stood from the chair at the bedside, leaned towards the medical bed to she switched off the holonull connected to Steven's bed, she walked towards the exited of the room, as she opened the door she looked back at Steven. "Do you want cream or sugar?"

A few hours later, Steve felt well enough to sit up and a conjured a layer of light that slowly flickered into another low resolution holo-cloth jumpsuit and picked up the cup of coffee and took a sip, then returned it to the tray. Steve scrunched up his face to the now cold coffee, as though it was a bitter taste.

Moments later Byron and John returned to the medical area to check in on Steve.

"How are you feeling?" The John inquired through the COMM. "Like I can stand up to the gravimetric pressures of planet Wells" Steven answered.

"Good, I got us a ride home, I am sure your family is worried about you" John asked. "I'm sure they are" Steven said as he attempted to slowly stand from his medical bed, once Steven got his bearings, and the room had quit spinning, he walked to the exit of the room, pushing the open door button and headed out to the asseveration room where John waited.

The three men then walked out to a hall of the medical treatment room, as they walked Byron showed an image of the remains of the Solid Luck as a hologram that hovered above his hand. Several crew and special vehicles had already arrived to clear the wreckage, and mend the facility.

As he displayed the site a beeping noise came from his arm, Byron closed his hand effectively closing the image out, and quickly swung his arm in front of his as if to give an invisible man a left hook. He lifted his head, looked at both me, and excusing himself; he pulled the message up from the back of his arm and studied the content closely for a moment, then turned back to the other two.

"John, Steve, the techs say the Hassar robot they took in had an unstable form of static memory and it was erased when it was deactivated, so unfortunately there was no useful information that could be extracted. The rest is firmware and that's all basic programming, so there is no way of seeing who the target of the attack was." the Commander said regrettably, as he lowered his head, and asked to be excused to get back to his duties.

The two continued down the hall until they made their way to a transport counter.

"Gentlemen, your transport has arrived," a young lady said from the other side of the window. "Lucy! How nice to see you again, how is the intern position treating you?" John said. "Hey John, it's good, I am sure getting extra credit for doing so." Lucy, looking behind John to see Steve following him. "Steve... Steve, Are you alright? I heard about what happened" Lucy asked. "I've seen better days but I am sure I'll make a full recovery" Steven said with a smile.

"Good, good, I can't believe that your son Chris has asked me to go to prom. It would be just like a double date with Justin and Nicole," Lucy said.

"Well, that's great. Who else in your group is going?" John asked. "Well, Eric, Tyson, Shelly, and my brother Josh," Lucy stated. "Well, that's great. Can you please lead us to our transport home?" Steve asked. Lucy smiled. "Alright, come on I'll escort you there." She lead them down the walkway to the smaller transport vehicles.

CHAPTER THREE

HOMEWARD BOUND

The destruction of Earth caused a lot of grief, but people now had to make a new home on other planet. Not many of the planets could support the mass numbers that once inhabited Earth, such as Mars. Mars, which was Earths smaller neighbor, had less gravity than Earth. Most buildings, homes and facilities had huge gravity generators to simulate Earth's gravity.

On the other side of Mars, New Joseph, Ute, U.S.A.2., There was a vast cornfield where two young children were playing in the evening, the large ultraviolet lamps that hung above rained their rays across the landscape providing light that the sun could not provide being so far away to grow the much needed crops around the Martian world.

The Children's mother Tara Haysting, Steven's wife, standing five feet eight, her sandy blond hair, shoulder length, her skin slightly orange from the vast amount of iron in the food, water and air that blown around the Mars atmosphere sat in her mobility chair to kept an eye on her children, she sat near the rear of the family's home, she scoured the news about the attack on the Solid Luck, and saw that John and Steven were injured, and found a current article that read that her husband was released from the medical unit, and was on his way home.

Though the orange or even red skin that from the exposure to the Martian soil wasn't the only side effect of the human's new home world, something the planet had an unexpected effect that even the doctors don't know what caused, and the nanites couldn't heal, but Tara was paralyzed from the waist down. Tara had begun to lose the use of her legs around the age of thirty five, and in the short five years lost all ability to use them at all, however some lose their ability to walk, or other lose other motor functions, and some earlier than their thirties; this condition was deemed the Martian Syndrome. Because of the Martian syndrome, Tara was depended on the use of a mobility chair to get around; sadly this was an all too common occurrence for all the young women who reside on Mars, starting with the first female pioneers who settled the planet after the terraforming took. Tara was now slowly starting to feel the weakness spread from her legs to the rest of her body, and she knows it would only be a matter of time before she would be totally immobilized. There is only one known treatment for the Martian syndrome that is successful, to leave Mars, and never return, but this is not an ideal solution for everyone, for space stations, and all the space craft in the human fleet of this time cannot support the new booming population now rebuilding on Mars.

Because of the Martian syndrome women are encouraged to marry young, and have a family before their twenty fifth birthday, though because the mass loss of population from sickness and death before man-kind left the Earth, large member families are also encouraged, to replace humans population.

"Viking...Lander...Viking...Lander...Viking!" One of the two small boys left the cornfield. "Satellite out of orbit." "Ah man, how did you know?" "I had a hunch. I got you, you're it now!"

"Sam, Curtis! It's getting late, and your father will be home soon." Tara called to her children. The two young children heard her call them in, they ran towards her, and entered their home through the kitchen entrance at the rear of the house. In the span of a few minutes after they retired inside, a small bulky craft resembling a cross between a charter bus and a helicopter with no blades flew overhead and landed. The small craft sprouted Landing struts that continued to lower until the craft touched down on the outskirts of the corn field. Steven's home was off in the distance from the field.

A ramp descended as Steven stood before the first step, then stepped down to the lower step, and continued onto the red soil and paved walkways that lead around to his home. Steven then turned back towards the cockpit. "Thanks for the lift!" Steve shouted waving his hand. The transport retracted its ramps and then lifted high into the air drawing in its landing struts, the small vessel darted off in another direction to return John home.

"Daddy, Daddy, you're home!" the two younger children cried, as they saw Steven, their father entered the home from the front foyer.

As Martian homes go, this one was recently built custom homes, having the most up-to-date designs and technologies. It had a sunken den and hall that led off to four bedrooms. Next to the den was a kitchen that led to outside. The main entrance from the foyer came into a family room just before the den.

As Steve came through the hall to the den after coming home for a long couple of days at work, Tara, came to comfort him. "Oh dear, I heard about the terrible accident with the Solid Luck. I saw the VIDCOMM, and you were carried away on a stretcher... Come and sit down." Steven bent over to kiss his wife, but she raised the height of the chair to meet him halfway, and collided harder than they both liked, but having this happen before, figured that this will happen again, and ignored it, and were just appreciated that they were once again reunited and embraced each other, Steven's chest pained him as they hugged, but it concerned him only as a minor nuisances, as to showing his wife his affection was his more important that his comfort.

Tara led Steve to an overstuffed sitting chair that reclined, and encouraged him to sit. Tara accessed the entertainment part of the home network when two of the four poles with bulbs on top that lined the walls of the den lowered, projecting a realistic holograph image of the news, the image made you feel as if the reporter was standing in your living room. A tall brown haired man that was neat, clean shaved, and perfectly parted hair stood in a shiny suit not eight feet away from where Steven relaxed in his recliner.

"As we continue to watch, we want to thank you for joining us tonight, if you are just tuning in, I am Bryan Wilcox, as we continue to reported about the earlier incident, a mining maintenance ship the Solid Luck was struck by a Hassar intercept ship, then exploded after crashing into it. It seemed that the attackers were caring explosives. Six onboard were killed, several were injured. No report yet of whom why the Hassar ship was sent to attack the Solid Luck, it's been almost two years sense that last attack from the Gillenium Council, no word from the Gillenium Council for the reason of the attack.

A dark haired woman with tan skin and a red skirt and a white waist coat entered as if to join the reporter and Steven in the room with a large smile "I am Amanda Foster, and Later tonight, a mission from G.O.D. well not exactly, but the company Ground Organic Development will be doing a live broadcast and a special report, 'Restore Earth'" the holograms continued to chattered as Chris entered the den seeing his father relaxing. "Father, hey, your home, are you ok dad? I saw what happened to the Solid Luck, are you okay?"

"Chris, I am, just a few nicks and scrapes, I am ok." Chris came over and to give his father a big hug and squeezed, in which his father released a loud groan.

"Are you alright?" Chris asked as he pulled away suddenly hearing his father in pain.

"Yeah, nothing a few hours of rest wouldn't take care of." Steven laughed. "How is school?"

"It's, ok, Justin keep abusing me at school" Chris complained.

"Were you stealing his fries again?"

"Everyone is making a fuss; no he offered them to me!"

"Oh, you forgot to thank him, then?"

Chris just snorted, shook his head, "Big fuss, I'm not going to tell you about how the low gravity basketball tryouts went." He said as he marched into the kitchen to forage for a snack. Justin from his room poked his head down the hall to the den, seeing that the recliner was occupied, and not by Chris, Justin hurried through the hall to greet his father.

"Hey dad, I heard the fuss, how are..." He snickered as he said that.

"I heard that!" Chris shouted from the kitchen, which made Justin smile a little wider as he looked up towards the kitchen door.

No turning his attention back to his dad, "How are you feeling? Are you alright?" Justin asked as he greeted his father. "Hey Justin, I am a little sore. I should be fine in a couple of hours. How is school going?" his father asked.

Justin, who was eighteen, currently attends the Red Sands social School. Justin and his friends all attended the school together including his girlfriend Nicole. Social as interactions with others, Justin who was roughly five feet and four inches tall, parted brown hair on the left, and dark green eyes, Justin had suffered from a high iron issues because of the high concentration of it in the soil, making his skin a tad red as if he was flush.

Justin responded, "Great dad, I am really starting to understand interactions with business, many forms of dance, and I have just started socializing with current event topics, and the self-defense class is teaching us sword play" "That's great, son," Justin's father said.

"Are you still doing the object projection from your palms?" Steven asked.

"I am, do you want to see?" Justin nodded his head.

"Sure, show me a few."

Justin held out his hand to display a cube that morphed into a ball, which then turned into a cone before Justin closed his hand.

"Fantastic, I wish I could do all those, I am lucky just to materialize an interactive display screen"

Justin then decided to join his father and sat on the love seat near his father to watch the news.

Steven thought to himself after hearing Justin go on about school as though Justin was missing, Justin and company had more adventures, and was very independent, and now he is as if he saw the same from Justin as he did with the machines he maintained on planet Wells, and wanted to encourage Justin but how?

"Dinner time, Come on you guys; I slaved over a hot keyboard and screen to fix dinner, come on, and wash up," Justin's mother called as she came through the door kitty-corner to the sunken den as the corner of her mobility chair pushed the spring hinged door open that lead to the kitchen.

Justin sprung up from the love seat, as well as Steven who put the recliner in its up right position, and out stretched his arm. "Justin, will you help your old man up?" Were just came around, and pulled his father out of the chair.

The two then lined up to enter the kitchen, Justin patently waiting behind his father.

The kitchen, almost square, had a very futuristic design; there was no stove and no fridge, none that was recognized at any rate. There was no real dining table, unless commanded, as with the chairs. Along the wall were three screens, and two odd keyboards. Text on the first screen was moving from side to side as a list of instructions for servants, chores and other tasks that need to be accomplished was displayed. The second screen was a calendar showing dates and times. The third screen was showing recipes, and other instructions. Tara's Mobility chair hovered higher to so she could reach the keyboard, and touch the tip top of the screen, if needed.

As Steven and Justin entered the kitchen, they held their hands out, palms up, while a disembodied robotic arm that protruded from the wall sprayed a bacteria killing mist, and then flashed a UV beam over the palms of their hands, killing germs and sanitizing them. Shortly after Sam and Curtis entered, doing the same having their hands sprayed, and flashed as they entered.

Now the family standing around the room they anticipated the chairs to rise from the floor so they could take their seat.

"Oops, I knew I forgot to do something," Tara smiled realizing now that she needed to raise the kitchen table and dining room chairs from the floor. Once fully extended the family pulled out their chairs and took their place around the dinner table to eat.

Justin's family owned several robots; two of the robots were activated, and were ordered to enter the room from the corners of the kitchen. The robots were circular bases with an accordion mid-section and a cylinder on top, as the two arrived, the mid-section expanded reviling two arm like appendages with dexterous fingers on the end. The two robots approached a large metal food processor near the work station of the kitchen; The first one extended its arms which took hold of a large tray of food, then delivered it to the kitchen table, placing dishes and bowls in front of the family, then followed by the second one setting drinks and a pitcher in the center of the table. The first robot then returned with an empty tray, placing it on top of the food processor. The food processor spat out another tray of food in which the first robot once again took to the table. After the last tray was placed on the table, the robots then quietly returned from their starting point below the floor and powered down unless needed.

The family started dining as the last of the food was placed in front of the family. Steve commented, "So, they're trying to re-terraform the earth again." He laughed. "Isn't this the fourth time this year? If they keep trying won't they blow up the planet?" Tara said with a grin. "Well, the special report will be on soon, I have to write a report on it for current events," Justin said.

After dinner the robots re-entered the room from below the floor, and proceeded to clear the table while the family entered the den and sat comfortable. Justin and Chris lay on his chest on the soft carpeted floor; Steven held Sam, as Tara held Curtis while sitting on the couch. The family turned their attention to the special on terraforming Earth. All of the poles around the top of the room slowly lowered, and the lights dimmed ready to project the evening's entertainment. With such a device there was no bad seat in the house, and it almost seemed as if you were there in the midst of the image. Justin ignored the image and continued to practice his holo projection palm skill with more complex objects.

It is important to note that at the point when Earth had become uninhabitable the population made a mass migration to the stars. Around the Earth's orbit, large space stations were erected to accommodate stragglers, to those who either unable to venture out to the other worlds, or those who did not want to leave the planet far behind. Most of the population attempted to populate other celestial bodies of the Sol solar system. From Earth's moon to Pluto, a small stake was made at an attempt for a new life; a popular place was Mars, though smaller than earth, many warmed to the red planet. The population struggled to call the new settlements home, despite the lack of resources such staples were needed to provide a stable environment for growth.

Mars being Earth's neighbor, and closest in size held the highest possibility of sustaining life, therefore it was chosen as the Second Earth. So after two hundred years a proper footing was made, terraforming possess were quick, and held up better than was expected, even with the overwhelming and overabundances of iron found in the Martian soil, crops and farms were started with special greenhouses and hydroponics'. The Martian diet consists mostly of soya for proteins, for meats were scarce, but there were plenty of leafy greens and other plants. Milks came from many plant sources, and all non-fruit sugars were banned including corn and sugar beets, but corn as a food source was still a viable option.

Mars size which is noticeably smaller than Earth, therefore Mars has less gravity than Earth, so people know they have to be constantly active and to exercise excessively in case they were able to return to Earth one day. Most buildings, homes and facilities had huge gravity generators to simulate Earth's gravity so that it's not necessary, but figured there was nothing wrong with being in great shape as well.

The family was alerted of a visitor when the doorbell rang, a side screen next to the door showed a picture of Nicole. Curtis Jumped from Tara's lap screaming "I'll get it" as Sam did the same shortly behind. Justin trying to pull himself from the floor, looking up from his palm, and as the door slid up, Justin's palm emitted a pink heart. Nicole walked towards him, and when Justin realized the object he was projecting he quickly closed his hand and blushed.

"Oh, how cute! You're getting good at that. I am having trouble just making a box. Can you make the heart again?" Nicole said with a smile. Justin shook his head, and blushed again. Nicole kissed Justin on the check. "Please?" Nicole asked smiling. "OK, just for you." Justin opened his hand, and a blue patch of fluid was pulled tighter into a formless mass, which he slowly changed into a red color.

He glanced up at Nicole, and once again the pink heart appeared. He thought it would be romantic if he acted like he was going to blow it to her. He started to blow at it. The heart moved toward Nicole, then expanded and faded into the air around Nicole. The two came together for a big huge, and then kissed.

The two walked towards the love seat to sit down, Justin turned to Nicole to ask her if she wanted some water to drink. She responded by nodding her head. Justin projected a holographic tablet from his hand, and connected to the house network to call one of the robots, which he asked to bring two glasses of water.

Justin's two younger brothers started singing. "Two love birds, sitting in a tree, K-I-S-S-I-N-G. First comes love, then comes marriage, then comes baby Justin, in the baby shuttle!"

Justin tried to grab his brothers, but fell off the couch and landed face first on the floor. As he lay on the floor, a message was displayed and a representative approached the middle of the image. Justin quickly got up and sat back on the couch to take notes. A robotic servant extended its arms out to give both Justin and Nicole glasses of water.

Once again the screen flashed with the special announcement from "the Restore Earth Special". Seeing this special, Steve motioned the display to raise the volume so the family could listen to the announcer.

An older gentleman in an environmental suit, holding a glass and metal helmet approached a pulpit with several microphones attached at the top. The name Rob Gibson rep. of G.O.D. displayed at the bottom of the broadcast.

"Ladies and gentlemen." Rob spoke. "I regret to announce that yet once again, G.O.D. our organization, has been unable to make this planet, the planet we all know and love, once the home of the human race, Earth, a place to inhabit. I started this assignment nearly six years ago when I over saw a field trip from a school from Mars. Green grass and a few flowers were blooming, it was spontaneous, and I saw what the Earth was, and what it could be again, so I decided to take charge of helping out nature. Although G.O.D. cleared off a great deal of the pollution on the surface, brought in rich soil form other worlds, and filtered the air, nothing again will grow anywhere, and we do not know the reason why," the representative said gravely.

A reporter approached the pulpit. "Is it because the planet is two hot, could it be global warming?"

"No, too cold, but we can't seem to find what has cooled down the planet, and has affected the core too, now slowed to an unsafe level, with the core in motion it created a magnetic and gravimetric field around the surface of the planet, but now the dead planet allowed almost all of its oxygen, and heat to escape into space, this is also the same reason why Mars was so difficult to produce and livable atmosphere, but on Earth we have injected large amounts of carbon dioxide which is a fertilizer into the air, we have tried to suspend water vapor in the atmosphere by melting the ice caps, The water molecules that would reflect the suns light and build up heat around the planet, but the temperature still drops, water still freezes, and is too cold for life to live here, now."

"But that doesn't explain why islands in the oceans are currently covered by the ocean, why California, New York, Maine, or Florida are currently under water, half of Texas us submerged, or the disappearance of Cuba." The reporter badgered Rob from G.O.D.

"Actually it can, the ice around the poles expanded it displaces the water of the oceans, water expands as it freezes, and this is why there twenty feet of ice covering Australia." Rob explained.

Another reporter approached the pulpit. "Rob, are you and your organization still going to attempt to restore the Earth to livable conditions again?"

"As much as I love the Earth, I have a great group of volunteers, and would very much to see the Earth living and breathing again, I am afraid that I am going to have to dissolve the Ground Organic Development movement, this was out last attempt. Thank you everyone for your support." Rob said tearful eyed, as he turned from the pulpit lowered his head, and walked towards his colleges who also had tears streaming down their cheeks, With a large group hug, the group walked off view of the media.

A spinning screen came up that said "This has been a Restore Earth Special.".

"It's a shame. My great grandfather told me about leaving, and what it was like to move from one planet to the next," mother said, with a look of disappointment.

Justin and Nicole looked at each other, now coming to realize that six years ago was where they had met, on Earth, on that very field trip; it was a very special field trip.

Steven pondered for a moment, that his son and his friends needed to get out of the house, or at least Justin, and Earth as good a place as any.

"Justin, when was it last that you went to the Earth?" Steven asked.

"I guess almost six years ago, why?"

"Have you wanted to go back?"

"Hey, go back, great idea," Justin said with a smile.

Nicole looked at Justin. "What are you thinking?" "Earth, I know, let's take a trip to Earth, what if we go back to where we first meet from that field trip..." Justin explained. "I want to come too," Chris said excitedly. "And I suppose you want to bring along Lucy as well?" Justin asked. "Well... I hadn't thought of that. Does that mean yes?" Chris replied. "Why not? Let's invite the whole gang to join us," Nicole said without missing a beat. "Then it's settled," Justin's father said thinking this may be the activity that gets Justin out of the house, that makes Justin, Justin again, and if it gets his friends involved, the more the merrier.

Justin's intentions were misleading and not exactly what he had in mind. He was hoping more for a romantic getaway, and now it was going to be spoiled by all these invited/uninvited teen guests. Even though Justin agreed, he was secretly disappointed and grabbed Nicole by the arm and took her aside.

"Nicole, I was hoping that… Well..." He blushed and choked on his words. "Well... I was... I was just hoping it would be the two of us." "Oh Justin, you're so cute! Maybe next time. Let's go have fun," Nicole said smiling. She gave Justin another kiss. Justin blushed again, and walked away towards the couch. Nicole called to Justin. "So when do you want to go?"

Justin looked towards his father and mother, who gave Justin a look of approval. Justin, put a semi-smile on his face. "What about, the day after tomorrow?" Justin asked. "Really?" Nicole responded. "Yes, really. Well I guess if there are more of us there, we could stay longer too," Justin thought out loud. Justin glanced at his father, who nodded with a smile.

"Great, then let's tell the group. You get a hold of Tyson and Josh. I'll get a hold of Eric and Shelly. Hey, tell them all to meet us at the mall on Diemos tomorrow near the landing bay, under the birthing of Justin Haysting," he said.

"What about Lucy?" Chris asked. "What about her?" Justin asked back. "Aren't you going to invite her?" Chris responded. "No, you are, she's your girlfriend," Justin said, becoming a bit irritated. "Oh, I never thought of that," Chris replied, puzzled.

"How long do you think we will be gone?" Nicole asked.

"A fortnight," Justin said, looking back at his father, who once again nodded.

"Two weeks sounds ideal" Steven said putting his hand on Justin's shoulder with a firm grip, and big smile, and returned to the couch to sit beside his wife.

Justin turned back to Nicole. "Well? We'll be back within a week before our final prom." He said loudly, pulling Nicole close and then whispered in her ear, "Maybe we'll even get married shortly after." "Really!" Nicole screamed excitedly. "Shhhhhhhhh...." Justin said waving his finger over his lips. "I don't want this to get out quite yet, but yes," Justin whispered, looking over at his father.

After giving the trip the go-ahead, Justin's father had said, "I think it would do the group some good to get out of the house, and what more of an excuse could they need than going to Earth. On, around Earth there are many people. Granted, they live in environment domes, or on the stations, there shouldn't be any problems. I think that the Light-hawk is the right way to go since it could certainly fit twice as many people as Justin is traveling with. He should have fun."

Later that evening Nicole used a mobile travel application to request a transport home, she lived quite a ways away, so she left early so she could get ready for school the next day.

CHAPTER FOUR

TELLING THE OTHERS

The next morning Justin and Chris got ready for school. Justin walked to a panel next to the door in the kitchen and tapped a few keys. A robot came out went to the food processor, that delivered a tray with both Justin and Chris's morning meal. Both Justin and Chris received a breakfast bar from a tray along with two odd glasses that had a middle divider between some juice and a milky white substance. Both glasses were sealed with a thin plastic cover so the two halves would never mix. Justin picked up the bar with one hand, and the other hand picked the glass up, peeled the milk side with his teeth, and tilted his head back, quickly drinking the milky fluid. Justin made a sour face, then peeled the rest of the cover off and slowly finished off the juice. "The juice makes it all worthwhile," Justin said as he bit into his breakfast bar and exited the kitchen.

Chris took the glass, peeled both sides, rotated the glass so the divider was running up and down, and quickly drank both fluids at the same time. He wiped his mouth with his arm, and laid the glass on its side on the tray. He laughed as he took the bar, and watched the robot try to balance the glass, and then try to catch it when it fell off the tray, although Chris didn't stick around to see what happened when it landed. The glass shattered, at which point small air vents opened in the floor, pushing the glass around.

A wind funnel was formed, which sucked the glass into a metal cylinder that lowered in the center of the ceiling, once all the glass was collected the cylinder raised back into the ceiling. The wind funnel also picked up the robots tray, keeping it in place till the suction stopped. The tray fell from the ceiling, hitting the robot square in the head knocking it over.

Chris ran to catch up with Justin and in the low Mars gravity, pushed off with his feet, Jumped over Justin, and Shelly landing behind the two.

Justin and Shelly who were chatting about meeting up in school, took notice as Chris kicked up the red soil, and coughed as they tried to wave to dust away from them.

"You dust-hole, your staining my outfits!" Shelly said as she flickered her holo-cloth skirt around her to brush off the dust, now resetted her outfit looked brand new. Justin following Shelly's lead also flickered his holo-cloth jumpsuit, and matched Shelly's outfit colour scheme of gray with blue trim out lining his pockets and waist.

"But you saw that, I got at least seven feet." Chris said excitedly.

Justin and Shelly talked as they walked towards the bus stop for the Red Sands social school. The sky was almost gray with bluish colour from the large manmade reservoirs that held much of the planets drinking water. Chris followed a ways behind them trying to jump even higher. "Shelly, OK, so I know we have been meaning to do get out, have a group activity for a while, but Nicole and I, well it was her idea..." Justin was trying to speak, but was interrupted. "And my idea too," Chris blurted out as he landed near the two again.

Angrily Shelly and Justin flickered there holo-cloth again after the dust settled.

"OK, and Chris's idea too. But what I am trying to say is that, were planning a trip to the Earth," Justin said unconvincingly.

"Why? Oh, I get it, I saw the report too, you want to try and help G.O.D. restore the Earth?" Shelly accused them.

"No, that's...that's where I first met Nicole six years ago, and I think it would be good if the group got out and get together again, besides school. It's been a while," Justin said, now trying more desperately to convince himself it was a good idea to invite the whole group.

"Alright, I am in, Earth may not be the most ideal locations, but as long as there is a swimming pool, I am there!" Shelly commented while Justin seamed deep in thought.

The bus arrived, the bus was an old modeled transport shuttle painted yellow, and there were four rows of seats that could fit twenty-five. It lowered itself to the ground, and a set of steps descended from the door. The sudden landing of the bus woke Justin from his trance like state as Shelly pushed Justin on board. Followed by Shelly, and Chris was last as the hatch slammed behind him making Chris jump into one of the two rows of seats. On the bus Chris sat, seeing his uniform was dirty he flickered his holo-cloth, for the pants sleeves were stained red from the Martian soil.

Nicole was already on the bus and gestured for everyone to sit near each other and for Justin to sit next to her. As they walked between the first rows of seats, they sat; a bar above them lowered putting a cushioned beam across their stomachs holding them into place.

"So, did you tell them?" Nicole asked. "I tried, but Chris kept interrupting..." Justin tried. "No I did not," Chris once again blurted out.

"See, what did I just say? You know I could just leave you at the lunar customs, without Lucy..." Justin said angrily. "No please don't, I'll be good," Chris pleaded. "Then quit interrupting," Justin said. "OK," Chris agreed quietly. "And quit kicking up the dust, I don't want to reset my jumpsuit image again." "Okay brother." The four continued to talk on the flight to school.

The Red Sands Social School: Babies at birth are given all knowledge shortly after birth in the form of nanites: the tiny machines are injected into the baby's body, altering the body from the immune system, and healing, as well as giving it unlimited access to knowledge, and so Schools are only for training, and socializing. The Red Sands was one of sixteen of such schools that littered the small Earth neighbor Mars. The class rooms were small, and most of the classes were taught with holograms called Holographic Education and Academic Retaining Teaching System, or H.E.A.R.T.S. pronounced Hearts, though the school had more than four hundred of them, they were referred to by their serial number. Most of the units were kind but strict, and could speak to each individual student through their COMM units.

The small yellow transport landed on a special pad that extended from the side of the schools dome like structure. After the children departed the transport jetted off allowing the next transport to do the same. The triangular pieces that made up the dome were held in place by a large frame. The triangular pieces held structures and rooms, one or two held fields, and had a central gravity generator. Moving from triangular piece to triangular piece was done by a small four person shuttle, colour coordinated for each destination of the same colour.

As the group was freed from their lap beams they made their way off the bus just in time to hear the first of the early bells ring.

As Justin approached the Shuttle ramp his COMM announced that it was switching to "School mode" knowing that only school facility members or the Hearts would be able to communicate with him. The other four heard the same as they followed behind Justin.

The group split up to go to their first class in different shuttles with other students who exited their transport, but before leaving to climb aboard their own shuttle they made plans to meet again at Justin's homeroom.

Later that day before Justin started his homeroom period, Eric and Tyson joined the four, and Lucy snuck in with a holographic display, Lucy made it appear as though she was clutching it with her hand, information wildly flashed across the display.

"How is your father, Justin?" Lucy asked. "He's fine. A little stiff but I think he'll pull through," Justin answered with a smile. Lucy smiled back. Barging threw the door Eric blurted out to Justin, and the class. "Earth Earth Earth Earth, travel... Where? When When When?".

Eric, age 18, had suffered a malfunction with the nanites that affected the speech center of his brain, so he spoke in odd sentences, sometimes backwards, or he just spoke in ways that didn't always make sense most of the time. What he lacked in communication however, he made up for by being one of the most profoundly talented programmers ever, and can even speak it flawlessly.

"Eric, were trying to decide that, but tomorrow is what we're aiming for, so tell your parents, were going as a group, and my father is allowing me to barrow the light-hawk.

Eric nodded vigorously, and then took a seat near the group.

Another one of Nicole's friends, Rachael entered the homeroom and sat with the group. "OK humans, what's going on?" Rachael asked. Chris laughed at Rachael, and every time she says that, as she says it quite often.

The group tried to talk all at once. "OK, everyone please settle down," Nicole said rising her arms.

"Everyone, Nicole and I, well, we're planning a trip to the Earth. Chris wants to invite you, Lucy, and Nicole wants to invite everyone else," Justin said to the group.

A look of shock came over Rachael's face. "Like always, I have to keep you humans out of trouble" She whispered to herself. Chris over heard her again. "Has she not looked in a mirror?" He thought, but then turned his focused back on the plan.

The bell rang beginning the class period.

"We'll talk about this later at lunch. Until then," Justin whispered.

Shelly, Chris, Lucy, and Nicole rushed out of the room off to their own homerooms; Rachel still stunned located an empty set, and sat down shaking her head from side to side, Rachel knew however if Justin and his friends didn't go on this adventure she would never exist.

A holo projection from head to toe lowered in front of a large display screen, a woman with short sandy blond hair in a three piece dress, her features were young, but showed signs of wisdom, the number 137 in block numbers was written across her forehead, her iris in her eyes were as the rainbow colours, and slowly spun around her cornea, though from time to time her eyes would take on one colour depending on her process.

"Class today is on speaking in front of crowds and large groups. We will cover socializing, current events, and other subjects of interest...." the teacher rambled on as her eyes turned green before turning back to the colour wheel.

If one didn't know any better, no one would have believed she was a hologram.

Justin was then called upon to deliver his report of the "Restoring Earth special report"

"Justin, please deliver your report on the events from last night, please" 137 asked.

Justin calmly walked to the front of the class, there were less that fifteen students in the room, but was still enough to make just fill he was delivering an important speech.

"G.O.D. or ground organic development had seeked out restoration to our beloved home, many believe that the mess on Earth was cause by man, and man also attempts to clean it up, but the damage is far greater than what man could have done, and far worse that man could attempt to repair. Because the loss of the Earth, man as a whole has had to come together, to work together to better ourselves, and create new homes together, the new homes may not be as robust as Earth, so we must maintain peace to maintain our homes. Because of the special report last night, I often think back on the events that took place almost six years ago on a field trip I took, and where my friends and I meet for the first time, and to mark the occasion, I have invited my friends to embark on a subsequent journey, journey back to Earth, back to where we first met. I also encourage, if you are able to rise to the challenge to venture your way to Earth, to see mankind's origins, I assure you, you will not regret it." Justin pressed his hands together, and bowed towards the class, raising back up, he slowly pulled his hands apart"

"Very good Justin." 087 commended Justin, then turned to the class. "Please give a round of applause class for Justin."

The class clapped for a moment, and then 087 turned back to Justin. "So when are you planning to return to the Earth, soon I hope."

"Well we plan to leave tomorrow as soon as possible," Justin said with a nod.

Nicole was in her holo projection class on the other side of the dome structure. "Nicole, hold out you hand," the Hearts 204 said as her eyes turned a light blue.

Nicole held out her hand.

"I would you like to try and form a box for me," the teacher commanded, then smiled as her eyes a darker blue.

Swirling light, with shades of purple and light black slowly formed into a box shape with some masses sticking out of the sidewall. Nicole tried to concentrate harder. She held the box tight for a moment, and then with an explosion the image was gone as though it turned to liquid and puddled down the side of her hand.

"You had it for a moment. An excellent display none the less. A little more practice, focus, I assure you, you'll be able to keep that form longer, and not let distraction interrupt your image. I've just been informed that you, Justin and a few friends are going to Earth, is this correct?" The teacher asked.

"It is, what are your thoughts?" Nicole with a reassuring smile.

"Well I think it's an excellent idea, and I am sure with the five day journey to Earth, hopefully you can squeeze in some time to practice making holographic forms, Justin would make a great tutor too."

"Sure, assuming we can find some alone time too."

I am sure you will, you may have a seat miss. Parson, Greg can stand up for the class and make a sphere for me, please?" the teacher said.

The first lunch bell rang; the holographic teacher said her good-bye then promptly disappeared. As Justin got up from his seat the call assistant Miss. Anderwon, stopped him.

"Mister Haysting, I heard that you are planning a trip to Earth tomorrow, and that you are going to be taking a handful of the other students," Miss. Anderwon said looking down at Justin. "Y...y...yes I am... What's… Is something wrong?" Justin shakily responded.

"No, nothing is wrong, it's just that, well, my great grandfather told me of the last few years of being on Earth, and the heartache of leaving. I know you were born and raised on Mars Justin, but Earth was such a loss, and the uncertainty of where to go… I am sorry to keep you from lunch, but I just wanted to say, enjoy your trip. Bring me back some holovids of your travels," Miss. Anderwon said ambivalently.

Nicole, Eric, Chris and Lucy met for lunch and started talking. "So Nicole, where is Justin? I thought he would be here by now," Lucy asked. "I am not quite sure. He is usually here before everyone else is," Nicole answered.

"I hope he's not in trouble," Chris said glancing around the room. "Trouble? No no no no, Justin Justin's not in trouble. He he he he he he is here," Eric said with a smile. "Where?" Nicole, Lucy, and Chris said looking in the direction that Eric was looking. "Oh, he's getting lunch. Guess he'll be here in a few seconds then," Chris said.

Justin walked up to the table and pulled out a chair, setting his tray of food on the table.

"I am sorry I am late guys, Miss. Anderwon was just wishing us a pleasant journey. Now let's get down to business," Justin said.

Chris reached across the table to steal a few of Justin's fries. There was a loud, "Smack," followed by, "Ow, hey I was getting a few fries!" Chris looked at his hand, red from being slapped. "Sorry, bro. Reflex action," Justin said with a smile. "No that's abuse," Chris said with a dumb grin on his face.

Lucy smacked Chris on the shoulder. "Don't even think that. Your brother is good to you, and you know it," Lucy said with a smile. "No, not you too," Chris replied.

"Beside bro, if you wanted some fries, just ask, or distract me. Besides, you can have them," Justin said to Chris.

Chris reached over to take the basket of fries. "Smack," on the same hand as before.

"Hey, what was that for?" Chris said drawing his hand back with an angered look on his face. "You forgot to say 'thank you'," Justin said with a smile on his face. "Abuse!" Chris cried. Justin, Lucy and Eric laughed at him, as Justin moved his fries over to Chris's tray.

"Well, down to business. I was hoping to gather everyone up at the Nexus Mall on Deimos tomorrow, and borrow my father's shuttle; we could be there in three days. Then we could stay there for two weeks, and then zip back. Now Eric, since you're out of school after this, will you hang around and tell everyone in the second group? That is your mission if you choose to accept it," Justin said with a smile.

"I I I I I...OK... I understand understand, and mission accepted accepted accepted," Eric said, raising two fingers to his brow.

Justin Picked up his tray and walked to a garbage receptacle, and dumped his trash into it, and placed the tray above the bin, followed by Shelly, Chris while waiting saw an old portrait of the first Red Sands class some one hundred and twenty years ago, Chris studied it quickly, as he never really noticed it before. "That girl looks like Rachael. Oh, there is a list of names here," The name list on the plaque next to the picture listed her as. "Well what do you know, her name is Rachael too, and maybe that's her grandmother or family member?" Now seeing he was left behind Chris quickly dumped his trash and ran to catch up.

As the day progressed Justin, Chris and Nicole left their second to last class and caught an early school bus back to their area to prepare for their journey.

CHAPTER FIVE

AFTER SCHOOL

"How was school?" their mother asked as Chris walked through the kitchen door. "Justin abused me at lunch," Chris said. "Were you stealing Justin's fries again?" their mother asked. "He had no reason to complain, I gave them to him," Justin said boastfully following behind Chris.

"But that was after you smacked me," Chris said with a half-smile, half frown. "Well I think you should quit worrying about the fries, and get ready for tomorrow's trip, unless you want to get left behind," Justin shot back at him with a smile, Chris ran towards his room with wide eyes, and a fearful look on his face.

As Justin rummaged through the contents of the kitchen through the workstation to see if there was an afterschool snack availed Justin's COMM beeped.

"Justin? It's Nicole."

"Hey beautiful, what's up?"

"I have most of my stuff packed, I'll have the rest ready to go when you pick me up tomorrow, I'll send the stuff over I have ready now, I just wanted to let you know it was coming."

"Ok, love you."

"Love you too."

As Justin got off the COMM with Nicole, a red and blue cargo drone was seen outside the kitchen windows causing the corn in the field to displace in different directions as it hovered over to the house.

Justin didn't image the size of the drone, it was the size of a one of the personal shuttles at school.

"She really couldn't have packed that much could she" Justin thought as he exited the kitchen to receive the delivery.

As Justin approached the drone, an electronic voice announced that it had a delivery for Justin, from Nicole.

"I am Justin" "I have one package for you" "Sure, go ahead and give it to me"

The side panel of the drone slid open showing a number of packages inside, two robotic arms furiously fish for the delivery, as both arms returned to Justin with a bright red duffle bag with white straps, Justin reached and took the bag by the center strap, and slung it over his shoulder, He could feel that it was full, and heavy. After Justin took the bag the other arm then held its gripper arm up as a holographic display showed package weight, size, and to sign at the bottom. Justin looped the strap over his shoulder, and started to leave walking towards the garage. "Ahem" The drone spoke, Justin turned back "What?" "Sir, I need you to sign" "Oh, right" Justin said as he saw the display, and walked towards the hologram, Justin studied the display then with his finger signed for the delivery.

Now satisfying the drone's requirements, it tucked its arms back inside, the panel closed then flew off to its next destination. Justin started to walk back towards behind the house to the garage. Chris as curious about what just happened, his hands full of personal belongings he wanted to pack onboard the Light-Hawk, moved towards Justin with his arms full of his possessions like a blanket and a pillow. "What's that Justin?" "Nicole's stuff." "What kind of stuff?" Chris asked funny, wanting to pry. "Nicole's kind of stuff, and don't even think of peaking, or I'll leave you at lunar customs!" "Oh, okay, well, what about you peaking, you have to see if it's safe, right?" "You know, you're right," "I' am"

"Yes, Lunar customs is too good for you" Justin teased Chris. Chris got the hint and followed Justin into the garage through a small door just right of the big garage door. As Justin entered he produced a small holographic display from his palm of his hand, and lit up the garage long enough to place Nicole's stuff on the gondola shelving that lined the walls. The shelf he placed the bag was near the Hawk with other stuff that Justin wanted to take as well on their journey; the Light-Hawk was still tucked away under its tarp patently waiting to make the long trip into the depth of space of sixty million miles.

8 a.m. rolled around and Justin's alarm went off. Meeting Chris in the Kitchen, the usual, had their breakfast prepared from the machines then headed out to the garage attached to the rear of the house to prepare the light-Hawk for the vacation.

Justin and Chris exited from the kitchen to the cornfield. Chris had an odd feeling that both of them were being followed as a slight wrestling coming from the cornfield, but as Chris approached the field. "Chris, come on, let's go, unless you want to be left behind, help me!" Chris struggled to turn his attention from the cornfield towards Justin and preparing the Light-Hawk.

Rachel lifted her head above the new stocks of corn spying on Chris and Justin. Justin approached the aluminum sighting garage door, and opened the doors viva holographic image from his hand connected through the home network. The two entered into building where tools were place all along the walls, and gondolas held necessities for taking the hawk out.

"Chris, help me remove the cover from the Hawk, please." Justin asked drowsily.

Chris returned with a nod, and walked to the other side of the Light-Hawk, and started to untie the cord to the cover, than pulled the corners of the cover to free it from its sheath. The two rolled the cover over the back of the sleek and beautiful ship their family possessed.

"Wow, look at this classic." Chris said as the side was slowly reviled.

"It is, cruse through space in style, better than one of those tiny training antelopes, they made me claustrophobic."

The Light-hawk, Steven's person space shuttle, one of two shuttles that Steven and John restored from when John served on board the Delta 451, the other is kept at John's house the old Martian observatory. The Light-Hawk were still sixty years older that both John and Steven, But were some of the first crafts to fly faster than spaceship, even what is on the market now, though it hasn't been used in four or five years, yet still hovers motionless in wait ready to take to the cosmic voyage again, The craft looks like a speed boat, or tear drop shaped, with four wings that can retract, as well as landing gear from below, the scooped lower back has heat sink vents, and front with tinted cockpit window.

On the side of the Hawk was a control panel, and extended the steps from the side of the ship, and opened the hatch to gain entry. Getting to the cockpit, Justin motioned toward the left, and sat at the control console and began warming the Light-hawk up and initiated the start up sequence.

"Chris, I am heading inside to get a few items, let's see if mom and dad are awake, and say our good-byes."

The two entered through the kitchen and found their mother and father sitting at the kitchen table. As the two went inside Rachel took advantage of the open garage and snuck onboard the Light-Hawk.

"Now remember the Solid Luck had more sophisticated sensors than the Light-hawk, but wasn't able to detect the Hassar ship, so be careful." "I will," Justin responded.

"We love you, both" Justin, and Chris's mom and dad said.

"I love you too," Justin said back, hugging his father and kissing his mom.

"And we love you too, Chris. Now don't give your older brother a hard time," their father said.

"Is it ok if I give him a hard time if he's picking on me?" Chris asked.

Steve just chuckled to himself.

"Well I better be off. I am sure Nicole is wondering where I am. Chris, I am heading out. Is all your stuff packed?" Justin asked.

"Yes it is in the garage. Let's go," Chris said excitedly.

Justin smiled, and put his arm around Chris as they walked back through the kitchen, exiting the house on to the Martian soil in route to the garage.

Even though Justin had his arm around Chris, Chris looked back to scanned the cornfield, after a moment looked back as the two approached the open door to the garage.

Justin's family came out to see them off, and helped move items from the gondolas into the hawk, once their stuff was packed, Justin and Chris said their last good-byes, and then entered the Light-hawk. Justin sat in the pilot's chair, as Chris took the co-pilot chair. Going down the start-up checklist making sure all systems were green and ready. Justin piloted the small craft out of his parent's garage, they could see their family outside by the edge of the cornfield waving, after fully backing out Justin raised the small craft above the garage, and piloted towards Nicole's house.

In less than twenty minutes of travel the navigation system informed them that Nicole's house was below.

"Justin to Mr. Parson, were just above your position"

"Good timing, Nicole has been getting the rest of her gear ready, I'll open up the dome, and you can set the Light-Hawk down next to her sister the Silver-Eagle."

Justin brought the Hawk down in inside the small observation tower. This observatory was the first erected on mars used for exploratory research, but now decommissioned and the Parson family moved in as to make it their home. The rest of the house was underground.

Both Chris and Justin got out of the Light-hawk, walked toward the entrance and knocked at the door. John answered the door; however Justin was expecting Nicole to greet them.

Justin was always a little intimidated by Nicole's father, for he had a stern commanding voice, one that Justin was not accustomed to.

"Oh, where is Nicole?" Justin asked timidly. "She is getting ready for the crazy idea that your father suggested about going to Earth, and I did speak with your father, he was rather keen on the idea of getting you, and your group out of the house for a while, I am not too sure about this, especially sense we were just attacked by the Hassar."

Justin smiled fragilely and nodded his head. "May we please come in?" John held the door open as the two entered, and he escorted the brothers down into the lower part of the house by way of circular set of stairs that twisted down to the living room. Justin had been many times to Nicole's house however Chris had only been a few times.

The distinctive "Clank, clank," echoed through the hollows of the house as Justin, Chris, and John entered the living room. "Justin, as you know, your father and I are great friends. I know you love my daughter, and I want you to be extremely careful. I remember your father and I once traveled in that rickety old Light-hawk, and that starship has been halfway across this spiral arm of the galaxy. It is faster than any commercial craft out there, so you guys have fun, and bring my daughter back in one piece, you understand?"

Justin smiled fearfully. "Oh… OK… I… I will."

Chris snickered watching his brother sweat bullets speaking with John. John looked at Chris sternly. "What are you laughing at?" John demanded.

"Nothing!" Chris answered startled.

"Good," John then turned his attention back to Justin. "Justin, my daughter is in her bedroom, go ahead and fetch her for your misguided adventures, however I expect to hear from her every night, I worry about her, especially when she is with you!"

Running off in the direction of the bedrooms, Justin looked back at John nodding his head as he ran full force into the living room wall just before the hallway. Justin was able to catch himself before he fell, corrected his footing he disappeared down the hallway.

John rolled his eyes, seeing this "I know, what are we going to do with him?" Chris said lightheartedly to John.

Justin continued down the hallway to the bedrooms, here he saw that Nicole's bedroom door was ajar. Justin snuck up to the door, and carefully pushed on the door silently to peak into the room, seeing Nicole working with a holographic fish. The fish she was designing was small, silver and blue, with big beautiful green eyes. Projecting next to her work station was an animated image of a white sandy beach, blue ocean water with rolling waves, and above the water were fluffy white clouds that remained motionless. As she was finishing the last fish, she transferred it to the ocean scene. Now feeling it was complete, Nicole took an illuminated glass rod and moved the ocean to wrap it around a holographic sewing mannequin. She worked her way around the image, and made sure that it connected in the back, as Nicole moved up the portrait she glanced and saw Justin standing there, then moved back to the corner of the dress, doing a double take, seeing Justin spooked Nicole, and realized she was being watched by him, embarrassed she quickly saved her work and then closed the program. "Justin, what are you doing here?" Nicole sternly said as she stood up. "Don't you know its bad luck to see the dress before prom?" she continued.

Justin looked confused. "Isn't that reserved for weddings, not proms?"

"Don't correct me…, Oh." Nicole started than laughed.

Justin just smiled and helped Nicole up out of her chair she sat in while she designing her prom dress, and wrapped his arms around her, and they pulled slightly away from each other, Justin snuck in a quick peck on the cheek. "Were ready to go when you are, where is your stuff."

Now fully separated, Nicole was able to take an invisible small suitcase behind the other side of the workstation, presented to Justin for inspection.

Justin took the suitcase, and unzipped it part of the way to peak in.

"Hey, what!... I mean" Nicole blushed "What do you think you're doing?"

"Taking a peak"

"Why?"

Justin couldn't help but notice, it was full of clothing, socks and other outerwear.

"Ah, Nicole, we don't normally wear clothes."

"I know, but I like to be certain that I'm covered, were going to be spending a long time with other friends, and just..."

Justin was getting the sense that Nicole wasn't confident in her ability to maintain he holo-cloth outfit, and quickly zipped the suitcase back up as not to further embraces Nicole.

Nicole struggled for a moment to come up with an answer then remarked. "Well, this is what I want to take, will you just humor me?"

Justin smiled. "Sure, anything for you love, come on the gang is going to be waiting for us."

Back onboard the Light-Hawk; Rachel felt it was safe to step out and stretch, spending forty minutes in a cramp location made her joints sore. Making her way out of the storage compartment surrounded by supplies, made her way to the hall just past the kitchen into the cockpit, she could see the interior of the tower that made up the observatory, and a very similar ship like the Light-Hawk.

"This wasn't in the report, did they took more than one ship..." Rachel though seeing the Silver-Eagle. As she noted the event, there was movement coming from the observatory entrance, from a couple of figures. Seeing this Rachel dove back into the storage compartment and securely locked the door.

John and Nicole's Mother Taylor Parson walked Nicole, Chris and Justin back to the Light-Hawk, opening the exterior hatch the three slowly entered as they continued to make their good-byes.

Chris climbed into the co-pilot said in the cockpit waiting for Justin and Nicole to finish to make their way to the next stop, the Nexus mall.

Justin and Nicole still lingered in the entry hatchway talking to Nicole's father and mother.

"Just remember Justin, one piece, and I want my daughter to make nightly calls."

"Oh daddy, that's not really necessary, besides, I know you love him, you cry every time you know were apart" Nicole said with a grin.

"Really" Justin said with a. "That much?"

"You two seam so much like, what your father Justin, and I, being friends, I already married a great woman and my best friend Taylor, I am just glad that you are able to love your best friend, both of you, Have fun you too,"

Justin turned to Nicole, nodded. "Yeah." Joyfully, then turned back to John.

"Just remember Justin, make sure she calls every evening." John said.

"I will father, I will" Nicole answered, than gave him a quick kiss on the forehead, then closed the hatch.

An hour of travel time later they reached their destination, although autopilot did most the work while the three occupied their time in the kitchen, when an annoying tone was heard throughout the Light-hawks sound system. "May we have your attention please? Welcome! Welcome to the galaxy of saving, and a universe of great buys. Welcome to the Nexus Mall on Deimos, the largest mall within fifty light years, large craft docking in Bay eighteen. Please follow the guidelines."

After the automated recording played, accompanied by some odd music, another voice came through.

"Thank you for choosing Nexus Mall, may I have your name and license number?" the voice boomed.

The three lifted their heads in horror that they had lost track of time. Justin scrambled to get to the cockpit to answer the call of the Nexus Mall.

"Large Shuttle craft, do you copy, may I have your name and license number?

Justin Finally reached the cockpit to send a reply. "Yes, sorry, I am here, I am Justin Haysting, and the license is K-E-E-P-F-L-Y-N," Justin responded.

"OK, the craft is registered with Steven Haysting, any relation?" the voice asked.

"Yes... He's my father," Justin said. "I am expecting a party already waiting for me."

"Understood, three of your members are already here."

"Great! Page them and let them know I am here," Justin said.

"I will, Sir, and again welcome to Nexus, welcome to a galaxy of savings" the voice said.

As they flew closer towards the small moon, there were signs and holograms. Music from inside the mall was broadcast inside the ship, and even a few advertising holograms were projected inside the Hawk as well, showing fashion models with holo-cloth designs, games, movies and even food.

Justin's favorite was an IO pretzel with lunar cheese served only in the Food Galaxy on the thirty first floor of the mall, and Justin had hopes that he may be able to have one before they depart for Earth.

"Computer: block holo ads. Notify me when I need to return to manual control to land," Justin commanded, getting frustrated with the junk that was coming through. The Computer beeped back confirming it instructions.

Once again a tone came through the ship.

"No more ads!" Justin said with his hand on his face. "Computer: open channel."

A familiar voice came on. "Dude, hey. Justin is me it is, Eric, How you you you do-in man man? Forward to to to to seeing you I I I I am looking!"

"Good to hear from you Eric. I'll be docking shortly in Bay eighteen, square ten. Can you meet me there? Plus we need a few supplies while we are here. Are there any supplies that you need?" "Yes yes yes yes yes, supplies supplies, get I I I I will." "OK. I have Nicole and Chris with me."

As the small craft entered the circular entrance imbedded in the rocky surface of the small moon. Justin took the helm of the ship and followed as closely as possible the guiding lights that lead him to his designated parking area. As Justin began his decent he could see other larger transports, although larger than an antelope shuttle the other ships made the Light-hawk seam small. Now that Justin landed, he began to briskly walk to the entrance of the kitchen section of the Light-hawk where he was greeted by both Nicole, and Chris. Nicole came over to Justin and who wrapped her arms around him gave him a kiss on the check. Chris witnessed the event. "Ohhh... Shame, shame."

Justin quickly looked over at Chris "You know in a few hours you'll be doing the same."

"Let's go check out the back of the Light-hawk and see if it's ready." Nicole said leading Justin by the hand back to the end of the ship.

Chris grimaced seeing Justin being dragged behind Nicole. "So… Well, I am the younger brother. I am supposed to drive you crazy. Well anyways, I have prepared two rooms onboard the Light-hawk. The women get one and the men get the other," Chris explained.

The door of the kitchen opened the three walked through the narrow walk way to the rear, and looked at the two rooms. On opposite sides of the narrow hall, looking in they could see that both rooms could accommodate four people. The interior was simple, the light blue carpet went under the bunk beds, and four chairs around a round table, and hidden compartments opened in the walls to store their luggage.

"Looks, good, I'll have to give you that, Good thinking Chris."

"Thanks Nicole, see Justin, Nicole likes it."

"Well I like it too, seems good enough, it will make the next two days pass incredibly fast hopefully." Justin said seeing the long journey ahead.

Three person cockpit Justin then sat down again and turned the chair towards Chris and pointed his finger at him.

"Great!" He smiled. "And no sneaking about, because I am the oldest I'll be keeping watch making sure no one sneaks out for a late night meeting with their girlfriend," Justin said, like he was laying down the laws. "If you two want to spend time together, spend it in the kitchen."

"Yeah right, technically speaking, isn't Tyson the oldest?" Chris said with a smile.

"Well that's beside the point. The point is, this is my idea, and dad left me in charge. I am the captain, and you must obey me, or I'll leave you on the moon when we go through lunar customs," Justin said.

Justin wasn't kidding either. He already had one plan ruined, He wasn't going to let his brother ruin another, but it wasn't a complete failure.

Justin stood up from the pilot chair, stretched and lifted his arms up. He knew he wasn't quite awake, but he also knew that would change when he started hanging with his friends again. Justin walked past both Chris and Nicole, to exiting the family shuttle, waiting for the Nicole, then Chris to exit. They both one at a time passed Justin, who closed the hatch manually, twisting a circular handle the Hawk was locked, running his thumb across an entry coder protected the Hawk, and walked into the Nexus mall through bay eighteens entrance. The entrance showed many signs, no firearms, no holo-cloth face masks, no hover boards, no shoplifting, and no walking on the walls or ceiling. As Justin entered her saw a familiar figure come around the bend.

"Justin, with open arms arms, my my my friend. So see glad to see see you I I I I again," Eric said.

"Eric, I see you made it on time, and the others?" Justin asked.

Shelly rounded a corner moments behind Eric through the concert and metal corridor that led to the mall. "Well I got the message from Eric. He was blabbering on about some sort of mission to Earth…"

The walls of the passages and corridor were plastered with ads, holographic images, and flashing light for store and product available only in the mall, and wouldn't want to miss out.

"Mission?" Justin asked to Eric.

"Join… Group group group group later; mission gave you you you me; message sounded… Thought it was was was a quest, or a uniting uniting, mission of course what what what what... What I stated, stating the group talk talk needed, I contacted… They are here here here here now, and journey onto Earth Earth Earth."

"Eric, we're here for pleasure, a vacation, and no missions? Unless your mission is to get away and do some sightseeing on Earth," Justin explained.

"Dead dead dead dead planet is not sightseeing, time time time time time time more spent on on why planet not not not fixable."

"Fixable? I'm not there to fix anything...." Justin interjected.

"Auh... Hum," Nicole stated suspiciously.

"Well OK, maybe something between me and Nicole," Justin whispered in a low voice into Eric's ear. "I am thinking of marrying her after the prom. But keep that low key. I want to tell everyone myself later," Justin said, with a hint of a smile.

A big grin stretched across Eric's face. He turned around and ran down the corridor. "Justin Justin Justin, Nicole Nicole. Wed wed wed they are going to to to to to! Wed they are going to to to!"

Justin smacked his hand on his forehead with a loud clap.

"Looks like I am going to have company at lunar customs," Chris said.

"Will someone stop him?" Justin said.

"So, what is this little adventure about, anyway?" Shelly asked.

"Well, Eric is right about going to Earth. I just remember meeting Nicole there for the first time, and I just wanted to go back ever since, and Nicole wanted our little group to go too. Earth is a long ways from home. It used to be home, but now most people's homes are scattered throughout the stars.

"So, that's it? It's a vacation, our home away from home?" Shelly said with a huff. "Yeah, it's just a getaway," Justin said.

CHAPTER SIX

ADVENTURE...MAYBE

"This isn't like one of your usual adventures. Remember that time we found ourselves near Alpha Prime? The Hassar weren't much of a threat, but we found a few and they chased us to that ice planet. We had Josh with us and he piloted us through the glacier. They were on our tail and we cut our engine. Their huge ship passed us, and the Hassar craft crashed into the ice wall. When we left the surface there were six of them and we turned our tail back. The spiral arm dropped out of LS and the Feds wanted to take us in but then the Hassar and the Feds ended up destroying each other's ships and we slipped away! Now those were the days!" Shelly said with a smile.

"Yeah, but now I just want to settle down. And no I haven't forgotten. How about the time that we found ourselves by that trading ship and they were compressing a wormhole and we found ourselves attending a meeting at the Gillenium Council? We heard their plans for searching Planet Wells for that legendary time machine, and we told the mining core what happened. It's been two years and the only Hassar craft was the one that attacked my father's craft," Justin said with a smile remembering good times.

At bay eighteen Tyson Showed up, as they included him into the conversation the small group started talking about Planet Wells.

"But don't you remember what happened to the first mining ship that approached that planet?" Tyson asked.

"Yeah it vanished for nearly forty years. When it was found, they said they had only just reached the planet moments before," Shelly responded.

"It's kind of funny that the planet was nicknamed Planet Wells after we found out about the time machine," Chris said with a smile. "Time machine!"

"Yeah, if I remember the Gillenium Council language correctly, 'Coreim ix nit wa: Time Machine on Planet Wells'" Justin said puzzled.

"Maybe we could search for that time machine. Think of it! A time machine. Could you imagine what we could do with it?" Shelly asked with excitement.

"No, we are going to Earth. Besides Planet Wells has been searched over and over. There is no time machine," Justin declared.

"Fine. Earth. Great," Shelly said, once again huffing.

Shelly, Justin, Nicole and Chris left the hangar bay where the Light-hawk was berthed. They walked around the mall, one by one bumping into each other, and all of them had to step over Eric who had collapsed on the ground from trying to tell everyone that Justin and Nicole were going to get married.

"Oh Eric," Nicole said, helping Eric up.

"It's really no big deal. Justin and I weren't planning this for months or anything. Right, Justin?" Nicole kicked Justin in the leg.

"Right! Right. What am I righting about?"

"I'll tell you later," Nicole said in a whisper.

"Oh, no big deal. Right. Surprise no," Eric said depressed.

As the five continued to talk they found themselves on level thirty-one in the Food Galaxy area and sat at the closets table to the IO pretzel stand near the entrance of the Food Galaxy. The others slowly started to trickle into the Food Galaxy sitting at the table, joining in the conversation. Josh and Tyson came together greeting everyone, then Lucy who Chris gave a big hug to.

On board the Hawk, Rachel looked at her arm to display the time. She had been cooped up in the Hawk for almost a twenty minutes sense landing; she knew her part, if only if she could get inside the mall. Exiting the small compartment, Rachel made her way to the hall. She was just about to release the hatch when a small slow flicking light caught her eye. "Security" "Security? What, oh, Justin must have set the anti-thief countermeasure, Guess I'll have to release them, then, how hard can it be, a stupid human did it, and with three hundred years of experiences… Why is the light solid now?" Rachel said as she now noticed the change in light demeanor, and the sudden hiss that came from the hatchway, sealing Rachel inside.

Justin who still sat at the Food Galaxy recovering from an IO pretzel with extra Lunar cheese, Justin was disturbed by a message that ran across his arm. He drowsily corrected himself from a slump position, and checked the words that ran across his arm.

"Okay everyone, The Light-hawk is in bay eighteen, square ten, Nicole, Chris, Eric will do a little light shopping for the trip ahead, I have to check the Light-Hawk, I'll be back shortly.

The group continued to move together as they left the Food Galaxy to the nearest lift to the second level. Everyone went from shop to shop, some just wanted to look around others like Chris gathered useful items. After they parted Justin ventured back to the Light-Hawk in the landing bay located on the first level.

Reaching the Light-Hawk Justin could see that there were red lights rapidly flickering around the hatch of the Hawk, quickly disarmed the anti-theft system with a swipe of his thumb, and opened the entrance.

The Light-hawk was dark, so Justin illuminated the opening with a light projected from his shoulder to have a look around. "Noting seems to be tampered with, maybe it was just a false…"

"Justin, is that you, a voice came from behind Justin in the cockpit."

Justin turned to see Rachel standing just inside the cockpit.

"Rachel, what are you doing here, we were supposed to meet at the Food Galaxy, how did you get in here anyways."

"I stowed away, and then I got trapped aboard."

Justin laughed at the thought. "Unlikely, anyways lets go meet up with the group."

Nicole slipped away to a shop near the group carefully watching to make sure she wasn't left behind as she looked at holographic projectors in the shop next door, The Store that Nicole had wandered into was called Display-Ware, with its holographical sign glowing, and slowly spinning. The store boasted with large holo-displays that: rings, belts, other tidbits that held a small but powerful holographical projector.

finding one that was reasonably priced, and disguised as a necklace. It was small and kind of flimsy, but it was enough to store one hundred dresses, and animated articles of clothing, including gloves that expelled fire. Excited about the find Nicole took the necklace to the cashier and Paid for it with some credits she save for a rainy day.

"Do you want me to wrap it up for you?" The holo-graphical clerk asked.

"it's ok, I'll wear it out, thanks" Nicole said as she smiled and slipped it over her head and attempted to find the group before being left behind. The group was blissfully unaware that Nicole had vanished walking to the next store when Nicole had hustled catch up.

"Hey you guys, leaving me behind." Nicole said as she ran towards them avoiding other shoppers, robots and kiosks that littered the promenade.

"Chris, Nicole, where are you? I found Rachel, and were ready to go." Justin said over Nicole's and Chris's COMM.

"Were on the second floor, and the group tried to leave me behind." Nicole responded.

"She took off to some jewelry store, so it's not our fault." Chris tried to explain.

Nicole was shocked that Chris had noticed that she had escaped.

"Well you shouldn't have left her behind, anyways, are you guys ready to go."

"I think so, can't think of anything else we need, Eric, anything else we need?"

"I I I I, good think think are we, here here here, the Hawk meet you you you will will." Eric tried to explain.

"Looks like where on our way back," Tyson said joining the conversation.

The Chris, Josh and Tyson ran seeing who could make it first to the lift, as Eric Lucy and Nicole walked behind shaking their heads as the three in front ran into other people, and tripped over a robotic floor cleaner.

Reaching the Hawk, Justin extended his arm. "All aboard! I always wanted to say that!" Justin said with a huge grin. "Chris, show everyone where they're going to be staying."

As Chris showed the others around, Justin began setting up to take off from Nexus mall. Doing a quick check on systems and fuel levels, he accidentally engaged the weapon systems, launching a short blast of laser fire. The beam hit the plasma field that shielded the hanger platform from the vacuum of space. The weak blast was harmlessly absorbed in the barrier, but didn't go unnoticed and triggered red strobe lights flickered on a nearby collision detector. Justin's eyes grew wide in horror, and he quickly shut all systems down on the Light-hawk.

"Justin, what are you doing? Everyone is aboard, and you're shutting all systems down?" Nicole asked.

"Right, get Tyson and Josh up here."

"What's wrong?" Nicole enquired.

"Nothing, I thought I let them handle things from here on out."

"Really?" Nicole giggled.

Tyson cam pelting down the hall followed by Josh, Justin knew the two worked well together sense the early days when they were trained on the antelopes and often paired together.

As the small craft took off from the area, Justin flipped on the COM system. "Attention passengers. guys, we are on our way. A course has been set, and we're now headed for the Lunar customs: Earth's moon. It will take four days, and we're away!"

The group cheered.

Three days into the trip to Earth, and a few more hours till they reach Lunar customs territory. The gang all squeezed around the dinner table in the kitchen to share stories, adventures, myths and legends. Shelly shared her story about appearing in a middle of a Gillenium Council meeting.

"What is that?"

"It's a galactic comity where members, made up of hundreds if not thousands of races, and they gather around in this humongous conference room it has spike pit in the center, and a stage just beyond the pit on the other side."

"They they see, you you you didn't, not not?" Eric asked.

"Of course not!" Shelly gloated. "I am the master of my cloak" Shelly continued smugly.

"Boo" Chris said frightfully, which startled Shelly, who quickly turned transparent, dropping her soft drink onto the table spilling it. The whole gang laughed. Shelly quickly made herself visible again, and snarled at Chris.

"Yes, yes, so as I was saying before being rudely interrupted, I found myself on one of the many levels of the council floor and used my COMM unit to record what they were saying, I later translated it when I got back that they were talking about a massive machine somewhere on the planet Wells, some sort of time machine, but it wasn't just a time machine, this device that can transport incredibly large objects across the galaxy."

"So is that why they're mining that planet?" Chris asked. "No, stupid, we need the resources," Tyson said looking at Chris like he was lost.

"Hey, Tyson!" Justin snapped. Chris smiled as Justin was coming to his defense. "Don't call my brother stupid, only I can call him stupid, isn't that right stupid." Chris's expression went from happy to a disappointed shock with his jaw hanging open. "I'm sorry Chris, you're not stupid." Justin apologized, "I'm sorry too." Tyson apologized as well.

"It's ok. So where on planet Wells is this hidden machine?"

"We we we we not know that that for sure. Never asked asked asked where Council by by by by by Gillenium," Eric said.

"You want to go ask? I sure they won't tell you if they knew, and that would be the last time we would hear from you ever." Justin remarked.

"Yeah but how do we know that they never found it? We don't even know what it looks like. What if it's cloaked?" Chris asked.

"Cloaked, cloaked," Tyson stated.

"Why not? It's not a bad thought," Shelly said, convinced now more than ever that maybe the Gillenium Council maybe going somewhere with the search.

"But I don't get it, how would the Gillenium Council know about this mysterious machine on planet Wells?" Tyson asked.

"I don't know, I must have missed that part of the conversation, but I do know is that the speaker was thrown into the large spike pit after an uproar from the council" Shelly explained.

The ship tipped from one side as an alarm went off.

"Hassar!"

"Stray asteroid!"

"Collision course with another ship!"

As panic struck the group they began to jump to conclusions of other dangers that lurked outside the craft.

"Stay here. I'll keep you informed," Justin said as he quickly stood up and rushed to the three person cockpit.

"No worse," Justin quietly said over the COM.

The gang looked frightened.

"Nicole, could please join me up here? Everyone else please try to remain calm," Justin announced over the COM.

Nicole stood up and slowly walked toward the exit of the dining quarters. Chris and Lucy cuddled up, as along with Tyson and Shelly. Rachel grabbed a support beam to hold onto, and Josh and Eric held each other, putting their heads together and closing their eyes. The ship began to shake. Nicole had trouble making it to the bridge.

"I am here," Nicole said looking out and seeing what appeared to be fire swirling around the ship.

Justin jumped up and held Nicole close. By then the ship was spinning and rocking rapidly. Then the shuttles lights and displays darkened, losing power the engine stopped. After what felt like an eternity the light sprang slowly as all systems were being restored from a backup. The couples slowly looked up from their embraces. Eric and Josh screamed as they noticed that they were hugging each other. As the other couples started to laugh, Eric fainted.

"I thought we were going to die," Josh said.

"Well before we do, invite us to the wedding," Shelly said.

The group laughed.

"Gang, you might want to come up to the cockpit" Justin said over the COM.

The group got on their feet and left Eric passed out on the floor. Shelly was the first to get to the cockpit. She entered the room looking at Justin.

"Justin, the funniest thing.... Oh my good asteroids!" she said in shock looking through the windows at the tunnel.

"What do you make of that, Shelly?" Justin asked.

CHAPTER SEVEN

DRAWN BY LIGHT

A tunnel in space of blinding white light enveloping the shuttle, and dragging it towards the direction of Earth, but Justin was uncertain if it was coming from the Earth itself as it was barely a blue dot from his point of view.

"I don't know, and there aren't any known wormholes within fifty light years from here," Shelly said, puzzled at the phenomena.

"Could it be artificial?" Tyson asked.

"I don't know, I've never seen any like this." Shelly responded.

"Well, we're stuck and it's pulling us in. I have tried fighting it. We're on a collision course to whatever it is," Justin said.

"Holy space weevil, what is that?" Josh said out loud.

"Will explain later," Justin said.

"How long before we hit Justin?" Shelly asked.

"At the rate of decent, about two days. The engines are dead, and we have a four-day life support, that is if we survive the crash," Justin stated.

"Crash?" Josh shouted.

"Not now Josh." Justin snapped.

"What about the COMM system?" Shelly asked.

"Dead. I am not receiving a single channel of traffic," Justin said depressed.

"We can't just sit here and do nothing," Tyson shouted, looking as if he wanted to pull his hair out.

"We're all going to have to sit tight and ride this out. I have a little repair work to do on the ship. From this monitor it looks as if we're getting some extra drag from one of the rear side wings. I am sure if I can correct it we can get some more stability and control if we were somehow able to be released from this grip," Justin said calmly as he stood up from his chair.

"Justin, what do you want me to do?" Tyson asked desperately.

"Let everyone know we're still having dinner together in the kitchen. Maybe Eric can program the sensors to pick up where it is that this beam of energy is coming from, and maybe, just maybe find a way of getting us away from it."

"Oh, understood, Justin. I'll go tell the group," Tyson said.

"For now though have them stay in their rooms. I don't need any of them getting out and alarming the rest," Justin said as he walked towards the door of the bridge.

Later that evening everyone gathered in the kitchen.

"OK, OK, OK, but he had this cast on his right arm, and Tom kept asking to shake his hand, and now that's why we call Tom 'no-shake'," Justin said laughing.

The rest of the crew sitting around the table started to laugh as well.

"Good. At least we can remember the good times we had," Justin thought to himself.

As the passage of time slipped by, the group still said their good-byes in the kitchen dining area, laughing and poking fun at each other. They knew it wasn't going to last, for the Light-hawk was going to collide with the anomaly in a few minutes and the group was powerless to do change the situation.

The group lost track of time telling old stories about school and other events that taken place, including what Eric and Josh did after the ship lost power. Justin found this quite amusing.

Justin looked at his arm, the time illuminated on his skin. "Whoa. Hey guys, we should be dead,"

"Dead?" all of them asked.

"Or at least touched down on something, maybe, I don't know, but it's been over thirty-six hours" Justin corrected himself not to frighten the group.

"Well unless we laughed ourselves to death first, I don't know why we survived," Chris said with a fragile smile.

"It's odd, the Light-hawk isn't swaying or bowing, so we must have landed on ground maybe, Justin, you're in charge here, go check it out and tell us if it's safe or not." Tyson said with a smile.

Everyone else laughed.

Justin stood up and ran to the cockpit. After reaching the cockpit, Justin glanced out the windows, not believing his eyes, the edges of the glass were coated in frost, and shaking his head Justin checked the outside temperature on a center display. It read negative fifteen degrees. Justin's jaw dropped.

"Were in so sort of large metal hall or corridor, its cold, like, freezing cold, I'm on my way outside now, I'll keep this line of communications open."

Justin then turned back from the cockpit to walk through the small hall, to the exit hatch.

Nicole got up from the table and walked to exit the kitchen.

"Where are you going," Chris asked.

"I, I, am going to go give Justin a kiss for good luck, be right back."

The group ew'ed at Nicole as she left. Exiting, she saw Justin tapping some keys on a panel.

"Justin?" Nicole said concentered.

"Nicole! Hey love, what's wrong?"

"Oh, nothing, can I talk to you?"

"What's wrong?"

"The outside, you it was cold."

"Yeah, it's below freezing, but the holo-cloth suit will protect me."

"Well, that's what I wanted to talk to you about, how long have we know each other?"

"Five, maybe six years, why Nicole?"

"Well, I have been keeping a secret."

"What, wait, the cold, bag of clothing, and I…"

"Yes… I have a hard time projecting a holo-cloth outfit, that's why I wear clothing."

"So, your concerned that if you have to leave the ship, you don't have anything to protect you from the elements, is that it?"

"Yes, yes." Nicole said as she hung her head in shame.

"Why don't you stay on board until we figure out where we are, or how to get out, and if we need you to leave the ship, we'll cross that bridge when we find it, until then just stay warm." Justin said grabbing Nicole by the shoulders and kissing her on the forehead.

Nicole raised her head smile at Justin and returned to the kitchen. After leaving Justin continued with seeing if the hawk was still intact. Justin approached the exit hatch a back panel closed behind Justin as he formed a light environmental suit around him. The door to the Hawk opened, Justin exited the Light-hawk to check, and make sure the shuttle was still intact.

Justin stepped out away from the Hawk, he scanned the area, the room was metal, metal floor, walls and ceiling, the ceiling witch was over thirty feet above him had a slight glow to it that allowed Justin to make out that some of the panels that covered the walls were pulled away on the corners, and large containers littered the floor, with odd alien markings. Some of the containers were stacked on top of each other, as well as some were knocked over with blue fluid spilled out over the ground. Ignoring this Justin walked back to the hatch.

Putting his hand on the side of the craft, and ran his fingers up to the edge of the cockpits window, he continued walking around the front nose cone. Justin walked about ten paces from the shuttle, and then looked back at the Hawk. "Yep, it resting on its belly, maybe I should put the landing gear down?"

Justin removed his helmet on his suit, and noticed that the condensation became visible; the tip of his nose felt cold, Justin took a deep breath in, and then exhaled. He was surprised that he could see his breath. Justin could fill his eyebrows stiffen as the moisture harden and some of the ice from his brow fell, into his suit, onto his skin giving him the chills. The sudden shock made Justin scream, dropping to his knees reaching into his suit trying to get the drop of ice, and quickly adjusted the suits thermostat, which cause more condensation to rise blocking his view. Justin attempted to wave his hand in front of his face to stave off the rising condensation, but it was fruitless, and decided instead to rematerialize his helmet just so he could make his way back to the hatch of the Light-Hawk.

Justin walked back to the entrance of the Light-hawk, and climbed back onboard, and addressed his friends waiting in the kitchen.

"We have landed, and don't ask where, but there is atmosphere, very cold atmosphere, and breathable air, its just negative fifteen degrees, and my breath froze to my brow. I suggest everyone use their environmental suit, it's going to be difficult, but not impossible. Well, we said we wanted adventure, now we've got an adventure!"

CHAPTER EIGHT

WHERE ARE WE?

"Alright, Adventure!" the group responded to this new information.

"What's out there?" Shelly asked.

"I'm not sure, containers, and wall to wall metal, and what ever lived here, must be incredibly tall."

"Tall?" Chris asked as he stood from the kitchen table.

"well the room that we are is huge, we could fit the solid luck in here and still have room to walk around."

The group gasped as they heard Justin's report.

Chris and Shelly hearing the news formed an environmental suit around themselves. Josh as well but geared up in an exoskeleton suit.

Justin leaned to one side in the doorway door way entrance to the kitchen. "Josh, I need you to man the helm. Eric, get the remote networking equipment. Let's see what we have gotten ourselves into." After giving instructions, Justin began to walk towards the cockpit.

"Awe, can I at least keep the suit on?" Josh hollered at Justin.

"Sure, just don't wear yourself out.

"Yes..." Josh whispered to himself.

Chris stood and started to walk behind Justin.

"Where are you going?" Chris asked.

"Cockpit, I need to put the landing gear down,"

"Aw… man, if you scratch the belly of the light-hawk dad is going to ground you when we get back."

"I hate to say this, but IF we get back."

Chris hung his head. "True," and nodded.

Justin activated his COMM throughout the whole ship. "Everyone, I need you to grab on to something supportive, you've been warned"

Justin flipped the landing gear to support the shuttle, as sections of the ship tilted, and corrected itself.

As the ship supported itself, Justin could hear a few things jostling about but then settled now that the ship was motionless.

"Systems, on-line they are. Triggered a docking system the Light-hawk has. I will see if I can free us from this place," Eric said in a confusing manner as he poked his head into the cockpit..

"Good work, Eric," Justin complimented, patting him on the shoulder.

"OK, everyone that wants to stay aboard, can, but I expect dinner when I get back!" Justin paused. "Only joking. We will stay on COMM and you can talk to us at any time."

Nicole, Rachel, and Lucy, stayed behind with Josh. Justin and Shelly took lead materializing their Holo-cloth environmental suit, while Chris tagged behind them doing the same. Eric on the other hand went the other way after he dawned his suit and to poke around the winding corridor. The corridor that led around to a large workstation some distance from the Light-Hawk.

With the holo-cloth, many tools and equipment could be created. Even lights could be projected from around the eyes, hands, or anywhere the user desired. Holo-cloth was only what was projected. The clothing was created by someone projecting an image, either in his or her hand, or over the body. It included a projection of the texture, or sometimes just an image. Many tools and pieces of equipment could also be created in the same way. The body would use holo projections produced by the nanites arranging the carbon molecules in the body's cells. A majority of the skin layers had holo nodes. The holo nodes also created an invisible barrier, so if the user desired a tool such as a wrench or screwdriver, the holo nodes would project a barrier shaped like such tool, as for clothing and armor, most clothing has no barrier, but in the case of armor, or environmental suit they are strong enough to stop a small high velocity rock in space, but not enough to stop a bullet.

Holo-cloth had some advantages, and some disadvantages. When projected, holo-cloth could create a vacuum-proof sealed environmental suit with a limited air supply, a limited exoskeleton, and even an umbrella for shade or rain. When the user was frightened, the holo-cloth would project a camouflage field, rendering the person invisible to the naked eye, and muffle the user's noises like breathing, and even walking.

Then there was the matter of what would happen when the user was knocked unconscious, passed out, or fell asleep. Since employing the holo-cloth took a small amount of conscious effort to sustain, the clothing, tools, and equipment projections would disappear, leaving the person defenseless and naked. Many new users wore undergarments, because they were still getting used to relying on the projection.

Justin shone his light along the path, looking at his COMM to make sure he had full signal.

Shelly tapped Justin on the shoulder.

"Justin, where do you think we are?" Shelly asked.

"I don't have the foggiest. We were being pulled into the Earth, but I can't tell if we were being pulled through phase or subspace as well, so who knows where we are. We could have even been pulled through time," Justin remarked.

"Well hopefully the place is as deserted as it looks," Chris added shakily.

At the end of the hall the three find a wall.

"Dead end" Chris stated.

"As much as I wish you wouldn't use that phrase, but it appears to be so." Justin answered.

Shelly rested he hand against the wall, it vibrated, and made a rumbling noise, as metal fragments rained down from the ceiling, the wall opened in the center. The loud rusty noise it made was a sign of years of lack of use and countless years of disrepair. As the door opened, the three noticed a tall dark figure. The three were stunned, and paralyzed with fear. Once the door fully opened the figure held out its hand as it walked towards the three. Both Justin and Shelly turned around and screamed. Shelly turned transparent. Even Josh who was monitoring all communications screamed and vanished. Lucy, Nicole and Rachel raced into the cockpit as they heard the scream.

CHAPTER NINE

GHOST SHIP... THE MANIX IV

"What's the matt... What is that?" Lucy, and Nicole screamed, Rachel was invested, but was unfazed standing next to the others.

Lucy, and Nicole continued to watch in horror as the enormous figure approached.

"Nav, ree, can, nax, ri, tive nac tox, nic, liz, ip wa, lare wick," The figure said.

Chris fell backwards on the ground and scooted as far back against the wall as he could and vanished as the figure drew closer.

"Justin, I don't think we're in trouble, but we're having communication problems," Shelly said to Justin.

"I agree," Justin said back to Shelly.

The figure began to speak.

"Welcome back Shelly and Justin," the large figure said, removing his cloak to reveal he was in fact a robot.

"What? Wait, how do you know who we are? And who are you?" Shelly asked, as Justin looked at the robot with utter confusion.

Back onboard the Hawk, Nicole Lucy, and Josh glued to the monitor with shock to realize that the figure was a machine, and that it in fact knew who Justin and Shelly were.

"Good, seams the timeline is complete, now I can relax for a bit." Rachel huffed, and then raised her voice "I'll be in the kitchen if anyone needs me." This startled the other three in the cockpit.

"I am the ship's maintenance worker and caretaker. I mean you no harm and have not had company for quite some time," the large figure said.

"How are you able to understand us so quickly?" Shelly asked.

"I scanned your brain waves, and your speech patterns are on file. I updated my programming to open communications, but I must say it has been some time since I last spoke...Human," the machine stated.

"Chris, you can come out now," Shelly laughed.

"Maybe he fainted?" Justin asked.

"Naaa. We would have seen him if he did," Shelly replied.

"Good point. Come on, Chris. I don't think it's going to bite. I don't even think it has teeth," Justin teased invisible Chris.

Chris became opaque again.

"It used to speak human?" Chris asked.

"I guess so," Justin whispered to Chris.

"So excuse me," Justin turned towards the machine. "Is there anyone else here?"

"Yes, you!" the machine responded.

"Me," Justin gaped.

"You!" Shelly gaped, pointing at Justin.

"Him!" Chris gaped pointing to Justin.

"Yes, if you are Justin Haysting," the large robot stated.

"Justin, he knows you. How?" Both Chris and Shelly asked.

"Millions of years ago… Wait, I can't tell you. It would ruin the timeline, especially if you're THEE Justin Haysting," the machine stopped itself.

"Am I still here?" Justin asked.

"Yes, as I said you are still here. You can even see yourself, but expect a shock. You may not like what you see, but I cannot tell you anymore further about yourself, so if you will, please follow me," the machine stated.

The four began to move down the hall.

"I am sorry I frightened you when I approached you. As I said before, I am one of a few of the last survivors of the original crew aboard this vessel. I am a robot; my owner's race was known as the Canero, and I am designed around their body form," the machine informed the group.

"Ah, here we are," the machine said.

The machine then placed its hand on the wall; a small square illuminated granting them access, in which the panels nearby moved upward allowing entrance to a new room where glass cylinders hung from the ceiling. All of them were empty except the last one, which contained a human body, torn very badly. The fluid inside the glass was frozen, the body kept alive until it has a chance to be fully repaired.

CHAPTER TEN

LIFE RUSH

Chris, as soon as he saw the body, threw up. Shelly put her hand over her face, and Justin crouched towards the ground, almost crying.

"No, no, no! Why? How? Am I...am I dead?" Justin said now supporting himself with his arms touching the metal ground.

"I am sorry. I cannot say anything further of the past, present, or future," the machine responded.

"Well, what can you tell me about this place? I mean where are we?" Chris asked.

"I can tell you. You are aboard the remains of a ship that fell into Earth's center during its creation," the machine responded.

Now looking up, and round the room, dark as the light from the hall poured in, Justin realized something "You said Earth's core, so, why, why is it so cold in here?"

"This is still near the Earth's core, yes, this ship was one of five, which was a means to escape, and find a new home, dive into suns to see if they would be stable enough to support a solar system like the one our home planet, when we found ourselves in your planet the coolant leaked into everything, it's also incredibly toxic, sadly there is more than a few hundred million gallons of this coolant that were disbursed when the ship eroded, and seeped into your soil." The machine answered.

"Really… really." Justin pondered for a moment.

"Was Justin aboard when this happened?" Shelly asked. The question made Justin forget about the coolant, and focus on the present, Shelly and the robot continued to speak.

"I am sorry, I cannot answer."

"Wait, didn't the special on the news, the president from Ground organic development say the planet was too cold to support life?" Justin trying to work out what went wrong in his head.

"Yes… So, Oh I see what you're saying" Shelly started to catch on.

"What, what are you saying?" Chris asked.

"The planet is lifeless because it's too cold, including the core of the planet, if we remove the coolant, the planet would warm up, and I wouldn't have to worry about getting the Martian Syndrome in eight to fifteen years from now." Shelly commented. Chris starting to understand now, his facial expression went from wonder to amazement.

"Unit twelve, is there a way to clean up the coolant?" Justin asked.

"Yes, it may take a long time, and the tools to collect and contain the leaked coolant are no longer accessible, but I will see if we can find a way to neutralize it, and make it inert."

Justin and shelly Smiled, though Chris still was a little confused.

Down on the other end of the long hold Eric and Tyson were exploring around several tall consoles that stood well above their reach. As they both worked hard to reach the top, the echoing sounds of screams that came from the Light-hawk engulfed them. Now deafened by the unpleasant vocals the two looked at each other, as they retracted, the equipment fell to the floor from their hands as they dashed off to the Light-Hawk to find out what was going on.

Now very much out of breathe from the sprint, and the struggle to move in the heavy suits that protected them from the harsh coldness, reaching the exterior of the Light-Hawk.

"Matter...What's...Going on...Hello," Eric said huffing.

Unfortunately for Eric, when he got panicky his words became even more jumbled, and misunderstand-able.

"Is everyone alright?" Tyson demanded.

"Eric, Tyson calm down. Everything for now is alright," Josh said to the two.

"Now...OK...What...Now...OK...Calm am I," Eric said, now a little bit more stable.

"Uhhh.... What he said," Tyson said with his hands on his knees, holding himself up.

Nicole, Rachel, and Lucy overheard the conversation.

"What did that spaz say?" Rachel asked rudely.

"Not sure, I am surprised anyone can understand him" Lucy stated.

"I guess they came in here to check on us, and Eric said he was OK, and well Tyson is just being Tyson," Nicole said, answering there questions.

"Whoa, she understands him," Rachel whispered into Lucy's ear, but Nicole heard it anyways.

"Yes, I can understand him," Nicole said angrily.

Lucy shrugged her shoulders.

Nicole walked from the room were the girls were staying, and entered into the cockpit.

"Eric, did you find anything?" Nicole asked.

"Yet...as..of...not, looking...finding, update...you'll...first...be," Eric said with a grin.

"We can't even find a computer screen. Nothing for access," Tyson said disappointed.

"it's OK, Justin and Shelly will get us out of this, they have been in worse situations," Nicole answered back.

"Scream...Scream, I heard...What?" asked Eric.

"Hey, I am just following Eric," Tyson said.

Nicole walked Eric and Tyson to the dining area. They walked to a side panel and pulled up the image of Justin in the cyro cylinder.

"Eric, the screams you heard from the Light-hawk were our reaction to the VID image," Nicole said as she brought up the image.

"Hey, he can't die yet, he still owes me credits," Tyson said in a semi-demanding voice.

Eric's eyes grew wide as he noticed the large gash marks along Justin's chest and around his neck and arms.

"That sure looks painful. Are we sure it's him?" asked Tyson.

"Dead... Justin...he...is?" Eric asked, with tears in his eyes.

"No, no. He is fine for the time being, and our Justin is still alive, exploring the ship," Nicole comforted them.

"Ship?" asked Eric.

"We're in some sort of spaceship?" asked Tyson.

"Yes, we're on an alien ship, and from what the scouting party has told us it looks pretty good for how long it's been here," Nicole said to Eric.

"Old...how you...know?" asked Eric.

"Yeah, are we talking a few million years?" Tyson said.

"Well it was here since the creation of Earth. I even think it was what wiped out the dinosaurs almost forty-two billion years ago. Would you like something to drink?" Nicole asked as she was walking towards a food-dispensing machine on board the Light-hawk.

"Yes...drink, please... Ship... this... Dinosaurs... wiped... out?" Eric asked puzzled, now lost in thought.

Nicole turned to him, and could almost see the gears turning.

"Sure, coffee sounds good. It may have wiped out the dinosaurs. OK, I'll shut up now. I am basically repeating what Eric asked, aren't I?" Tyson said.

Eric agreed nodding.

"Yes, it's OK, but yes, it's very possible. Here, I got you both a cup of coffee. Would you two like to talk to Justin?" Nicole closed her eyes, and held out a cup for Eric, and Tyson.

"Much....very...So, coffee...Thanks, Justin...talk...talk," Eric said excitedly.

"Thanks Nicole, Justin is a lucky man," Tyson said.

"And Shelly is a lucky lady for having you," Nicole added as she turned back to the image still being displayed on the wall of the dining room.

She put her hand near it to signal Josh sitting in the cockpit.

"Josh here. What's up Nicole?" Josh stated as he answered the COMM in the cockpit.

"Can you patch me through to Justin?" Nicole said smiling.

"Sure, here you go." The image of Josh shrank, while another image of a hallway was enlarged.

"Justin, a few friends want to see the living dead. Don't die on me yet, you still owe me credits," Tyson said laughing.

"That's not funny," Justin said angrily, the image quickly showing a very enraged teen.

As he looked, he saw it was Eric and Tyson with Nicole in the dining room. He laughed.

"Alive alive, you...are are are. Worried...me me me me...had," Eric said seeing a good friend still alive and kicking.

"Well what can I say? I have looked death in the eyes three times now, you know? Nothing like a near death experience to keep the blood pumping. Have you two made any progress with finding a way out?" Justin said with a fragile smile, knowing soon it might be his last.

"Not yet," Tyson answered.

"Then what are you two doing?" asked Justin.

"We're taking a coffee break," Tyson snapped back, and they all started to laugh.

"OK, well signal me if you find something. Justin out,"

After the COMM was switched off Nicole produced the necklace that she bought at the Nexus mall and gave it to Eric.

"Do do do, what you you you you, want me this with?" Eric asked.

"Could you please put an environmental suit in this to protect me from the cold outside?"

Eric smiled as he took the necklace to tinker with. Nicole then vanished from the kitchen to the cockpit to check on Josh.

The video feed switched back to the cockpit where Josh was sitting as he continued to monitor their activates.

"Do you want me to bring you something?" Nicole asked Josh.

"Yes ma'am. One coffee, a little cream, and a little sugar," Josh said with a smile.

After Nicole took Josh's order, Rachel peaked into the cockpit and looked at Josh.

"What's up?"

"I'm going to go catch up with Justin and Shelly." "Okay, I'll pass that along."

"Justin, you have a straggler trying to catch up with you." Josh contacted Justin.

"Oh, who, you mean… Rachel" Justin spoke, shocked to see Rachel walking around the corner in a suit.

"Yes, wow, she caught up with you that fast, what she do, power walk."

Shelly, Justin, Chris and the machine were Just exited the cryo room and sealing the room as Rachel joined them. The machine lead the way to the end of the hall that led from the area of where the Light-hawk was birthed. As the machine got closer the lift opened.

"We are going to take this lift here to the bridge of the Manix IV. It is the base of operations," the machine stated.

CHAPTER ELEVEN

CHANGE OF PLANS, AND TIME DOOR

A thin metal panel just to the left of the lift pushed opened and a small orb jetted out. Justin pushed Shelly to the floor out of the way, and Chris dropped to the floor as well, Rachel took note, but let it pass.

"We're all going to die," the little white orb screamed, bouncing off the walls of the hall. As it impacted the walls, sparks flew off the orb as well as debris dropped as though it was breaking apart.

"Don't mind that orb. It was once a faithful maintenance drone, but over the years its system slowly became corrupt, and it's now totally out of control," the machine said.

Justin directed the COMM away from Shelly.

"Josh!" Justin shouted.

"Yes Justin, what's the matter?" Josh responded, bored.

Josh looked up, and saw the small orb seconds before it crashed into the main window of the cockpit. Josh reacted as if it were a baseball hit through a house window, and although the little orb shattered the glass, it never broke through. The small orb now damaged slid down the side of the Light-hawk, crashing into the floor, the lights under it dome sides, and the two or three sensor lights flickered before completely going dim, as a small whisper of smoke rise from the center.

"Let me guess, you wanted to warn me about something," Josh said, displeased.

He uncovered his head realizing he was never in any danger but he was still a little shaky.

"Pretty much. Call Eric over and see if he can't do something about it," Justin said, laughing at Josh's reaction.

"Oh.. Ha, ha. Next time try to warn me a little faster," Josh said, a little irritated.

The machine ushered Justin, Shelly, Rachel and Chris into the lift.

"Whoa, this is huge! Especially compared to the hall. The hall could maybe squeeze the Hawk through, but no pilot would dare do that unless really necessary. The lift could easily fit both the Hawk and the Silver-Eagle in," Shelly remarked.

The machine introduced itself as Unit Twelve, and was one of three robots, and told them of the now two still functioning orbs still aboard the ship.

The four entered the bridge of the grand Manix IV, the room was triangular in shape. There was a table with odd shaped keyboards attached in the middle as well as consoles that circled around the large room. In the front of the bridge was giant screen, ever where along the bridge were odd arms that extended out and followed the explorers and Unit 12, displaying 3D information, stats and images of the solid rock outside projected from the ends of each arm.

"The massive screen you see in the front of the bridge here is also connected to something we call a matter transmitter, this screen can transport matter across the galaxy," Unit Twelve stated.

"May I try?" asked Justin.

"Sure," said Unit Twelve.

"Here is the access port for the coordinates," Justin quickly calculated the distance, The screen started to swirl, the red dessert of Mars, zooming in closer Justin could make out the homes, and neighborhoods, Justin recognized the corn field that his family is growing, the image pierced into the kitchen of his home.

"Unit Twelve, this is my home, I need to let my folks know that I am ok,"

Unit Twelve nodded. And with that, Justin walked through the screen and vanished.

"Master Justin, you are not due back from Earth for another three weeks, two days, and..." a servant robot said.

"Can it, serv!..." Justin stopped then paused to look back at the servant robot.

"Sorry, we're in trouble. Is my mom or dad here?" Justin apologized.

"Yes, they are currently here out back," the servant robot told Justin.

"Thank you. I gotta go talk to them," Justin said, quickly dashing for the back door. "Mom, Dad! Mom, Dad!"

"Justin, back so soon? Where is the Hawk? Something is wrong here. What's the matter?" the father said with great concern.

"I have no time to explain. The Hawk is trapped inside the Earth. I have seen my own dead body, and we think we figured out why the Earth is unable to support life," Justin said all in one breath.

"So, how did you get here?" the mother asked.

"There is a matter transmitter in a ship that the Hawk is trapped in. Come watch," Justin said, as he led them through to the den where Justin appeared.

"I'll try to get the Hawk back. We have no communications outside of the ship, no signal, but we will figure a way out. Give us two days. If we haven't figured it out by then I guess we'll have to dismantle the Hawk and bring it back piece by piece. We'll open the M.T.T. so you can send help too," Justin said before he promptly vanished.

Once back on the bridge Justin said to Chris with relief, "Chris, I told Mom and Dad of our situation. Don't worry, if we don't figure a way out in two days, then Mom and Dad will send for help."

Chris nodded feeling better that Justin was able to get the word out.

"Good news Eric and, I think I found a way out. A matter phase converter got us in here. I mean this is what dragged the Hawk in, and what can get us out of here," Tyson said, as he pulled another thin metal panel off the wall.

"Work work... Nice... but but but, work...does..it it it it? Out... us us us...get get?" Eric asked, walking up behind Tyson.

Tyson moved aside to let Eric take a look.

"We found it Josh, a way out...." Tyson said, not looking when he used the COMM.

The metal panel slipped, cut through many wires directly linked to the phase converter. This shorting out power for the hangar, and the open area glowed red then white, melting some of the surrounding pieces behind the panel, as the wires and the phase converter caught on fire, destroying their hopes of getting out.

"Or not. We're still trapped," Tyson said.

"OK, if you say so," Josh replied back.

"Damn!" Eric replied.

"Maybe there are more. Start removing panels," Tyson barked as he formed tools to remove bolts that held sheets of metal in place along the walls of the room. "Josh, Josh,! Are you there, Josh?"

"Yeah, I am here. What's up?" Josh asked.

"Any report from Eric or Tyson?" Justin asked back.

"Well, I talked to them. I think they're going to tear the alien ship apart," Josh answered back.

"What do you mean?" Justin asked.

"Well Tyson called me and told me he found part of the ship that could've help, and then... Well it must have exploded," Justin stated.

"Exploded? What are those guys up to?" Justin pondered.

"Maybe they're thinking of blasting our way out?" Josh said with a smile.

"Well OK, let's continue to keep this channel open, and if you get any communications from Tyson or Eric, patch me through as well. Speaking of which, can you patch me through to them now?" Justin said.

"What up, Cap?" Tyson asked.

"What did you guys find over there?" Justin asked.

"A device that can pull objects into their hold, and I think it was the one that drew us in."

"OK, hold on a second," Justin paused. "Unit Twelve,"

"Yes? Can I help?" Unit Twelve asked.

"How many of those devices do you have on board?" Justin asked Unit Twelve.

"We only have the one left. We have had to replace it more than its fair share of times. I am even surprised it was able to pull you fully in," Unit Twelve stated.

"Oh, OK, so maybe forget it. Can we move this screen down to the docking bay?" Justin asked Unit Twelve.

"Hey, wait Justin. We won't need to move the screen to the bay. We could move the ship to the screen," Josh said, thinking thoroughly about his actions.

"Yeah, but the device doesn't work, unless you want to fly the ship... through... the... ship... Hey, that might work! The hallways are large enough, and you saw that lift right?" Justin agreed with Josh's idea.

"Well I was only thinking if the robots could dismantle the ship, then reassemble it when we get to the bridge, we could, well, you know, fly through the screen," Josh said, again disappointed.

"Not bad, but I think if we retracted the wings, and everyone gave a hand, we could fit this through, and not take so much time to take the ship apart," Justin said, thinking.

Two panels opened on opposite sides of the bridge, and two other machines identical to Unit Twelve walked through. Chris dove behind the table, covering himself. Shelly, Justin and Josh all laughed at Chris.

"Intruders! Intruders!" the other two machines stated as they charged toward Shelly and Justin.

Shelly and Justin ran around the room. Shelly jumped over the table. With her foot she knocked new coordinates into the access port of the matter transmitter, and Justin ran straight into the screen, and vanished.

"Units thirty-six, and forty-two! These are not intruders, they are guests. Behind the table are Shelly and Chris, and the other behind me is Justin," Unit Twelve said, trying to get the other machines to stop attacking.

"We're friends," Chris said as he rose from behind the table with his hands in the air.

Shelly slapped Chris on the chest.

"What?" Chris replied.

"They're not going to rob you," Shelly said with a sour look on her face.

"Justin, you can come out now," Chris said.

"Justin!" Shelly called looking around the room.

There was no sign of Justin.

"Wait, Unit Twelve, you said Justin was behind you, but the only...object...behind...you, is the screen," Shelly said, thinking.

"No, no, he's...gone," Chris said, finally getting the picture. "Quickly. Check the coordinates of the matter transmitter."

"There are eight coordinates. The first is where Justin first went; the second is Alpha Major, a small asteroid; the third is Earth in the 22nd century; the forth is 18th century Earth; the fifth is 2nd century Earth; the sixth is the moon from 18 years ago; the seventh is...."

CHAPTER TWELVE

CAUSE AND EFFECT

A young student, in his messy small dorm room, typing away at his homework for the evening, held up a small crystal cube, and placed it into a dish, a laser beam bores into it as the student studies it closely. The room was three or floors up, a small window looked out over a college campus early morning, with light blue above and bright below the horizon. The brown shag carpeting seamed over two or three hundred years old, as well as when it was last vacuumed. A small double sized bed adorned either side of the room, with an elaborate series of tables in the middle.

Crrrasshhhh! As Justin bumps into a bookshelf knocking over a few knickknacks on top as he is thrown into the room.

"What the...Hey, how did you get in here? Did Brian put you up to this as some dorm room prank?" the student said, talking to Justin from his desk chair.

"No, I am sorry. I am lost, and I am trying to get back to my friends," Justin said, panicking and looking around the small room.

He turned around and started feeling the air behind him, knowing if he passed through where he was standing, he could get back to the bridge.

"What, I can't understand you with that spacesuit one, at least remove the helmet." The young man stated who had turned away from his desk.

Justin dematerialized his helmet. The young student rubbed his eyes in disbelief.

"Wow, what was that, and why are you swatting at my swimsuit calendar?" The student asked.

"Oh, her, she... is cute?" Justin said now looking at the calendar.

"Yeah, miss August; just doesn't stair the ink off the page will you." The student joked.

Justin slowly turned around knowing that it's impossible to stair ink off of a page.

"Well is there anything I can help you with?" the student asked.

"Is... it... cool, you know, if I... if I just hang here for a few minutes? Maybe I could even help you do... whatever it is you're doing?" Justin said nervously.

"It's cool. I am getting ready for an exam in a couple of hours on quantum particle acceleration, and crystal memory blocks," the student informed him.

"Crystal memory block? That's a pretty outdated technology," Justin muttered loudly to himself.

"What do you mean? Crystal memory technology will change the face of the world," the student almost shouted at Justin pointing to the dish with a crystal cube being bombarded by a laser.

Justin navigated the garbage and dirty clothes that cluttered the floors to approach the student's desk.

"No, no, the data transfer rates are too slow. Even if you got a pure sample, why not have an organic matrix?" Justin corrected him looking at the cube.

"Organic matrix?" The Student asked.

"Well the body uses cells, and the cells can retain more information besides their own DNA encoding, and thus information could be stored more readily..." Justin now realized and clapped both his hands over his mouth and walked back to the other side of the room.

"What's the matter?" the student asked, puzzled.

Justin, with both hands still over his mouth, was now shaking his head from side to side, and mumbling, "oh...no...no..."

"Oh was this a project you were working on? Maybe we could partner up. I am Sam Scotsman. Hey..., what's going on with your arm?" Sam asked as Justin's arm faded into the matter transmitter.

"Shelly, look! An arm!" Chris said as he pointed to the screen of the M.T.T.

Shelly ran over and pulled on the arm, to where Justin came through the screen. He then fell over Shelly with his hands still clapped over his mouth.

"Rachel, quickly. Shut off the transmitter!" Shelly said while still looking at Justin.

Rachel reached over the controls and powered down the screen almost bored like.

"No, no!" Justin moaned to himself.

"What, Justin?" Shelly asked.

Chris came over to help the two up.

"Who invented the organic memory matrix?" Justin asked.

"Sam Scotsman, why?" Shelly answered, looking puzzled.

"Well I met him, and just suggested the idea to him, not knowing who he was. Then he told me who he was, but even still, that was messing with time. It's bad enough an older version of me is in a cryo tube in a ship in the middle of a dead planet. I didn't tell him much, thank goodness!" Justin said with his hands over his eyes.

"Hey Justin, you'll never believe how helped get you back?" Chris said puzzled.

"Who?" Justin answered.

"No, go on, guess," Chris pushed.

"Bro, we don't have time for this!" Justin fired back.

"Ok, gees, it was Rachel, like she zoomed in on when and where you were like a pro," Chris pointed to Rachel who was walking towards the lift.

"Wow, and here I thought she didn't like all this adventure stuff," Justin said to Chris and Shelly, walked to Rachel standing next to the lift.

"Thanks for your help, for a moment I thought I was going to be trapped in the past."

"Oh, you're welcome." Rachel said as if it was no big deal, the lift doors opened Rachel got in by herself to take back to the Light-hawk, she stepped into the lift, and turned back towards the sliding doors, and hung her head. "Stupid human." She said under her breath as the doors closed.

Justin returned, and walked over to the table near the M.T.T. controls. He had noticed that someone had set their COMM there. He picked it up and propped it upright so he could relay a message to Josh.

"Justin, Shelly. Come here," Chris said.

Justin and Shelly approached Chris.

"Look, while you were working on a way out of this place with Josh, I found this. Justin, you said you were in the past talking to a Sam Scotsman, the father of the organic memory matrix, right?" Chris explained.

"Yeah, so?" Shelly said.

"So, you traveled through time," Chris said, trying to convince them of a point.

"So?" Justin said.

"Well the transmitter sent your signal to Planet Wells to send you back in time to Earth in the 22nd century!" Chris exclaimed, trying to get his point across.

"What?" Justin said.

"Where?" Shelly greedily asked.

"Well I don't know, but it just shows that the signal was broadcast there and then back," Chris stated.

"Wow, so the legend is true. It's true, there is a time machine on Planet Wells," Shelly said excitedly.

"Yes, as the ship was thrown into a decaying orbit by a large asteroid, the section of the ship broke off, but because our ship was damaged, we had no way of retrieving it."

"So, now we can," Chris said with a smile. "We can get it back. All we need is a way to find it."

Unit Twelve walked over to a computer panel, removed the siding from around the controls, and pulled out a small box, opening it revealed a small handle, connecting a display showing signal strength sat on top of the device. He unscrewed it at the center of the handle, then reached another hand into the wall and pulled out an even odder piece of tubing, with a hose-like attachment attached at the end, running the hose through the handle, and put a bulb found on one of the helms on the bridge, at the end of the hose then attached the loose bit of hose to the front of the handle.

"This will help you search for the missing pieces of our ship. Bring what you can to find it. It should have two machines, and a power generator matter phase device, allowing the ship to pass through objects much like what our tractor equipment did to your light vessel; the other machine the M.T.T., allowing passage through time, and space," Unit Twelve said.

"Nice," Chris said.

"Can we keep the M.T.T.?" Shelly asked.

"No," both Justin and Unit Twelve responded.

"Well there's nothing like wishing," Shelly said laughing.

"OK, find a way to get out of this ship. Find the time machine, and do not get killed in the meantime," Justin said.

"Agreed!" both Chris and Shelly laughed.

Justin, Shelly, Rachel and Chris took the lift back to the Lighthawk. The three were accompanied by the three maintenance robots that towered above them.

When the lift opened Nicole stood out front of them in a pink environmental suit and a big grin on her face.

Shelly was the first to emerge from the giant lift followed by Justin, who was amazed to see Nicole, and gravitated towards her, Then Chris and Rachel, followed by the Manix IV robots.

"Wha...Whoa, those guys are huge." As Nicole's face went from a smile to awe.

"You guys go ahead; I'll meet you at the Hawk." Justin said as he took Nicole to the side.

Nicole stumbled as she taken to the side, as she was infatuated by the sheer size of the robots. Now out of sight Nicole turned her attention back to Justin and smiled. "So what do you think?

"It's great; I am amazed that you are able to maintain it so well, so crisp and detailed. Are you comfortable, no condensation is escaping, are you ok?" Justin checking out her suit to make sure it's safe.

"I'm fine, no really." Nicole said showing it off.

"I knew you could."

"Well, not really, I picked up a necklace, and asked Eric to program it with a suit."

"Well he does good work and the necklace will hopefully holds up to long periods of use."

Nicole nodded her head as the two walked towards the Hawk.

The others walked through the hall, the eight made their way back to the Light-Hawk, with Justin and Nicole a little ways behind.

Justin tilted his head upwards towards the three machines. "Were going to pop inside for a moment, we will be right back.

Justin, who helped Nicole inside followed by Shelly, and then Chris behind Rachel, climbed aboard through the hatch.

Justin sat in the cockpit with Josh in the co-pilot's seat.

Other than the COMM all flight and navigational systems were dark, and cold.

"Well, let see if we can get the systems back online."

"Engaging anti-grav,"

"It's a no go, maybe our new friends can help?" Josh said as he flicked switches with no reaction.

After an hour of work, the three machines were able to undo the damage the device did to neutralize the Light-Hawks systems.

"Let's try this again." Justin said using his arm to support his body weight as he moved around the pilot seat to sit.

"Check," Josh said.

Justin accessed the COMM system. "Were going to try powering up the Light-Hawk, it might get bumpy, or nothing could happen at all, you may want to hold onto something."

"Go for anti-gravity systems."

The flight system lights lit up, giving readouts of power, and system attributes.

Josh Smiled. "Check" He said in a happy tone.

"Wings, retracting," Justin said adjusting some dials on a screen..

"Check," Josh said.

"Proximity sensors, online," Justin read off switching the navigation system on.

"Check," Josh said, knowing they were once again going to be moving.

"Chris and Shelly I want you two to walk in front of the ship," Justin said into the open COMM system.

"Aye, aye," both Chris and Shelly answered back.

"Eric, I want you to give me a heads up so we can address what going wrong."

"Sir...yes...do...will," Eric responded, then hustled towards the cockpit.

"Tyson can you monitor the thrusters?" Justin asked Tyson.

"Can do," Tyson answered back.

"OK, Josh..." Justin started.

"You want me to measure the anti-gravity output!" Josh interrupted Justin.

"Well actually no, I was going to do that. I need you to pilot this ship," Justin said.

"Really? OK," Josh responded excitedly.

The small ship began to move to the entrance of the basically straight corridor. Josh's strong point was being a pilot, but he misjudged the door, and the ship began to scrape along one side.

"Whoa, whoa!" Chris shouted as he saw the whole event unfold before his very eyes.

"Sorry, Justin. Hold her for a second," Josh said as he steadied the ship and moved the ship more towards the center of the giant hall.

"You're clear, now," Justin said, looking at the proximity sensor read-out.

The group managed to make it to the lift doors. Shelly already had begun to call the lift. The doors opened, and ran back to the hawk, and climbed aboard.

Justin guided everyone to sit in the kitchen. "Everyone, I think that just to be on the safe side, Nicole, Rachel, Lucy, Shelly, and Chris, I need you to follow the units and meet us up on the bridge." Justin instructed.

"Really, no way I want to be here with you guys." Chris responded.

"I just feel better if you were on the bridge; I feel it would be safer for you."

"Ok Justin, see you there" Nicole said understanding that this could life threatening.

"You too Chris, come on." Nicole said look at Justin's brother by the collar of arm sleeve.

"Oh, really, actual challenge and you drag me away… Sure, whatever" Chris grudgingly answered as the lift doors closed.

Now that the five had left and returned to the bridge of the Manix IV, once the lift had returned to the floor where the Lighthawk rested.

The doors to the lift opened to their maximum size, allowing the Light-hawk to pass through into the mighty space with little incident. Josh rolled the shuttle to its side to pass through the opening, spun the craft 180 degrees to face the way it came in then rolled back flat with the ground. The lift doors closed painfully slow, with enough time for Justin to quickly unbuckle his belts to the navigational seat of the hawk, made his way out of the cockpit, out the exit, he leapt to the floor of the lift and ran toward the door, with his arm stretched out press the bridge command on the panel. Then quickly leaping back to the entrance of the Light-Hawk, He was stopped for a moment as the elevator made its climb, Justin quickly getting his footing, returned, and strapping his belt in the navigation seat.

"Shelly, Chris, I need you to watch and guide us as we go to exit the lift so we can set the Hawk down on the bridge," Justin said over the COMM.

"Copy," Shelly replayed.

"OK, I am going to set her down," Josh commented.

The lift cart struggled to lift the extreme weight of the Hawk, then buckled, stopped, and hung for a moment. It was now a loud snap, could be heard, even inside the Hawk, The lights inside the lift went dark and then lift begun to drop at an alarming rate.

CHAPTER THIRTEEN

PILOTING A SHIP WITHIN A SHIP

Justin quickly re-energized the anti-grav system, the small shuttle, which was resting on the ground, but because of the rapid rate of decent of the lift, the hawk drifted towards the ceiling. The roof of the Light-hawk hit the ceiling of the lift cart as the anti-grav system stabilized, throwing everyone inside the Shuttle upwards. Shelly groaned as she smacked her head against a console in the seat behind the co-pilot, this knocked her out cold, her holo-cloth suit disappeared showing that she was now wearing a supportive undershirt and blue trunks. Josh looking out the cockpit, could only see his reflection in the window, switched on the exterior lights of the Hawk lighting up the inside of the lift.

Because of its awesome size, the lift's cart still dragged the Light-hawk towards the bottom of the shaft floor by floor, dropping faster. Even though the tiny craft upright the roof hull was rubbing the ceiling of the elevator cart this time, the group knew that escape was narrow. The remaining conscious friends screamed feeling the sudden uncontrollable drop. The feeling of weightlessness compounded with disorientation over took the crew as they struggled. The rapid decent in the shaft of the Manix IV had another adverse side effect, the group felt an enormous pressure on their chest, making it difficult to breath, and near impossible to talk. Tyson tried to divert power from other systems to keep the Light-Hawk a float and the lift from slipping further down the shaft of the Manix IV. The ceiling of the lift continuously banged again and again thunderously striking the roof of the Light-Hawk, Justin, Eric and Shelly Flailed about in their buckled seats, knocking Tyson out cold, losing the ability to maintain his holo-cloth, reviling he had worn yellow boxers with smiley faces.

"Justin... Justin Tyson is knocked unconscious." Josh said worried about his co-pilot. Justin struggled to breath, just shook his head then blacked out. Justin now out, his holo-cloth jumpsuit vanished revealing a white undershirt with a plain pair of red boxer briefs.

"Eric, Justin is out cold, I need you to see how far the lift shaft is, how long till we hit the bottom?"

"Justin, Shaft...the...two...long...miles, gravity... fifteen... artificial...minutes," Eric said, under the same effect.

"Do... Do we have fifteen minutes?" Josh desperate for answers asked.

"No..." Eric respond then passed out from the blood rushing from his head to his toes.

"Justin, Justin..." Josh said, needing to shake Justin.

Justin became reanimated now blankly looking at josh. Justin moved his lips, but nothing came out.

"Did your dad finish the laser emitters?" Josh asked.

Justin at this point could only nod his head before blacking out again.

Josh fought with the controls and spun the ship when he activated the laser, making several passes over and over again slicing through the lower half of the lift which separated, the lower half of the lift sped off, while the up half feel at a slower rate of decent with the hawk. Josh had the hawk in a hard tailspin, with the centrifugal force to much, Josh cut power to all systems. Now in a total free fall, the Hawk tumbled, scrapping the inside of the lift, Josh held on to the steering yoke trying to take back control of the Hawk, seeing Justin, Eric and

Tyson violently tossed about in their seats. Josh knew he didn't have long; restarting all systems was his main priority to restore control.

Chris and the other waited for the lift doors to open so they could take the Light-Hawk home. Feeling that it was taking too long, the quick journey up and down was brief. The group, except Rachel got worried.

Nicole felt the outline of her COMM attached to her chest just above her shoulder, contemplating contacting the rest of their group of friends. Seeing this Chris put his hand on Nicole's hand. "They're not answering, I already sent a message." "What does this mean? Unit Twelve what's going on with the lift?"

"Let me check." Unit twelve said, then made his way to a console, pulling a chair from underneath he had a seat, and accessed the state of all systems, though the face of Unit twelve was static, and all the units had the almost identical faces, of a elongated skull, and dual brows over it eyes, that had were shaped like sideways eights, thought a number of moving receptacles moved inside each eye, they mouth was a cosmetic piece that was expressionless, the others knew by the tone of Unit twelve's voice that the news was not good. "I am afraid Nicole that the lift crashed into the bottom, of the shaft; I am so sorry young humans."

Chris clutched onto Nicole, as she wrapped her arm him, and around Lucy. Nicole always felt sense meeting the Haysting family as an older sister especially sense Justin usually can get himself into trouble.

"No, no no, this can't be, That fooled human got himself killed and will take me with him, wait, if he did die, then why am I still here?" Shelly though to herself, then examined her arms and hands.

"No, no need for tears, their still alive," Rachel softly shouted, unattached but desperately to stop them from crying.

Josh Reaching, fighting the centrifugal force, the gravity from the tumbling ship, Josh remembered he was in the exoskeleton holo-cloth suit, and brought it full power to his arms and torso, stabilizing himself enough to kick on all systems. Pulling the Hawk out of the tumble, and now able to stop the top half of the lift. Josh felt a little more freedom in the control, and was able to angel the ship so the nose-cone was now facing the ceiling and with the laser cut the top of the lift.

"The laser is jammed, ok, I got this, if I spin the ship, I need to roll the hawk, hopefully, I can cut a circle large enough to pull the hawk out." Josh though, ordering the hawk counterclockwise.

"Ok everyone; hold on tight, it's going to get dizzy." Josh said knowing he was the only one to hear it, and took a hard right roll.

Josh cheeks and lips flapped as he groaned, objects in the cockpit flew around hitting him and the others, and loud crash noises of breaking dishes could be heard in the kitchen. An antique wood and metal clipboard and flight checklist smacked Josh in the face. Though it was a distraction it did no damage, and smudged a carbon copy ink print on his forehead and cheeks. Taking a moment Josh smacked the clipboard away, it fell towards the kitchen, landing with a wooden slap.

The laser continued to cut creating a path from the middle of the lift to the top; dust poured through attacking the Light-Hawk, which made it had hard for Josh to see through the cockpit window, already contending with a circular shattered spot from the orb. The laser cut grew, and at first first small rocks fell from the opened lift ceiling a few bounced off the Hawk, then larger rock rained down scratching the ship as they rolled down the sides of the tiny vessel.

"Well I guess that would explain why the elevator fell." Josh thought to himself as he piloted the tip of the hawk up, laser full blast to cut center panel freeing the Light-Hawk from the lift, the panel and rocks fell into the cart as it plummeted below.

Josh had enough control of the Hawk to wipe the sweat from his brow with his hand. Slowing the spinning, both hands now on the controls he straightened out the vessel, Josh pulled his other hand away from the control yoke to try bringing Justin around.

"What... What happened?" Justin asked.

"I cut through the roof of the lift, were free now, I'll get us to the bridge."

Justin shook the shoulder of Shelly after metalizing a simple jumpsuit. He noticed that that she had scratches and a bruise on her face; she slowly came around and looked at Justin.

"Justin? What's wrong, ow, ow." Shelly said as she felt around the bruise on her cheek. After she was through feeling her cheek noticed that Justin's lip was sliced in the center below his nose.

"We were knocked out when the Hawk lost control, and you banged your head pretty hard on the console" Justin explained, "are you okay enough to wake the others?"

"Sure, I think so." Shelly said as she turned towards Eric. Justin looked over the navigations.

"Where are we Josh?" Justin said trying to get a fix on their location.

"Were well below the hall we started out in, but we have a strait shot to the bridge." Josh said.

Shelly was crouched in front of Eric as he came around, as his eyes focused on her face, a worried look swept across his face.

"Bruise, okay, you, are, you a have?"

"Are you okay, you have a..." Shelly started to try to make sense of what Eric was saying. "Yes, yes I am." She touched her bruise. "I must have got this while we were passed out."

"Okay, am I, cut?" Eric said slightly panicked as he reached for his face.

"Nope, you seam fine," Shelly smiled, then took her seat, and strapped in.

Eric and shelly attempted to wake Tyson, but was unresponsive, so they just made him comfortable seeing that he was slumped over in his chair.

A large plum of dust engulfed the craft that made looking out the windows impossible.

"What's all this dust from, and why is the front of the Hawk so dirty?" Justin said as he peered through the cockpit windows.

"That dirt is from the top of the lift, that dust must be from the sentiment from the bottom of the shaft when the lift crashed into it, looks like were flying blind." Josh answered.

They continued slowly on their path to the bridge, and relied heavily on the computer and sensors for the location of their position in the huge shaft.

Justin pushed his COMM. "Justin to Nicole"

Nicole who was still trying to fight the tears, reached to her shoulder and tapped her COMM to answer. "Justin, you are alive"

"What… Yes, were alive, the lift dropped."

"We know, Unit Twelve told us that the lift crashed at the bottom of the shaft, but it was Rachelle that said you were still alive, how would she have known you were?"

"I don't know how she would have known, but were on our was now"

"I love you so much, be careful, how long is it going to take you?"

"I love you too, Let me find out" Justin said then turned to Josh. Josh looked back at Justin hearing the conversation.

"About Three hours" Josh he said with slow nods.

"Alright, we will make preparations here" Nicole said.

"Good, I love you, and can't wait to see you."

Reaching the door to the bridge of the Manix IV, by then the plum of dust had settled.

Josh took special care not to bump the ship into the walls, but did so once or twice before the dust settled enough to see the shaft.

Now reaching the top of the well, the crew of the Light-Hawk could see that the lift doors were closed and sealed from inside.

"Unit Twelve, you're going to have to open the bridge door manually," Justin said talking to Unit Twelve over the COMM.

"Will do. Are you guys alright?" Unit Twelve said back.

"Well apparently someone pressed the express down button," Justin jokingly answered.

"I saw the lift drop, and though you wouldn't have survived, I am glad I was wrong."

Everyone on the bridge gathered around the lift as Unit Twelve made his way to a panel near the lift doors and opened the doors to the bridge, just inside was the Hawk floating, the doors opened as far as they could, the group on the bridge stood to the right side of the open lift doors, as Unit twelve stayed on the left.

Josh brought the Light-Hawk about four feet onto the bridge before he set the Hawk down. Justin Eric Shelly and Josh unbuckled their safety belts, stood and made their way to the exit of the small shuttle, and walked towards the rest of the party. Nicole ran to Justin with arms open giving him a hug, as she stepped away Chris and Lucy approached Justin holding hands, and gave his older brother a hug, as well as Lucy. When the group saw movement from the opening in the Light-Hawk, Chris recognized Tyson who seemed a bit out of it.

"Tyson," Chris shout, running over he attempted to help Tyson from the Hawk.

"thought, wake, you never would up we" Eric said confusing as ever, as the rest of the group laughed, even Tyson had a good giggle.

Unit

"Unit Twelve, I guess this means good-bye for now. We will let our people know of you, and help you get your parts back," Justin said.

"Justin, here." Unit Twelve extended its arm out giving Justin a small plain metal box.

Justin lifted the lid to the box and pulled out one of many odd looking bracelets, Justin examined it for a moment, to see it was made of many thin bands of metal that were silver and bronze with a slip of metal on top.

"What are these?" Justin said looking at Unit Twelve, puzzled.

"They're bracelets with recall transmitters. They will allow you to open a gateway from anywhere to here on the bridge of the Manix IV," Unit Twelve responded.

"OK, wow, so we can come back any time?" Justin asked.

"Yes, any time, just swipe your fingers across the top, and it will transport you here. I had longed for company, and will be sad to see you leave," Unit Twelve said.

"Well I will try to return as often as possible, and I am pretty sure everyone else will as well... Wait, why don't you come with us?" Justin asked.

"I can?"

"You can, why not?"

"Then, I will take you up on your offer," Unit Twelve stated.

"Great! Gang, gather round," Justin told the group.

"Unit Twelve is going to be coming back to Mars with us, but first, some presents," Justin said still holding the box.

He opened it and passed out the bracelets.

"Put these on. These will allow us to return here at any time," Justin told the group.

The group was in shock and awe. They put the bracelets on, and commented on how cool it was to be allowed access. Rachel and Lucy however, wanted to leave the moment they arrived and didn't want or care for the bracelet.

"It looks tacky" Lucy stated to Rachel.

"Looks can be deceiving, we won't need one, if you don't want it, either way is fine" Rachel said which now confused Lucy.

The gang started to line up to board the Light-hawk.

Unit Twelve looking at the entry hatch to the Hawk, "I'm not going to fit, and there is enough room to walk around the hawk, and come with you to Mars."

"Justin, what do you want to do?" Josh asked.

"You fly the ship. I am going with Unit twelve through the open the portal to the surface for Mars. Set her down just past the opening. Unit Twelve and I will then pass through on foot behind," Justin ordered.

"OK," Josh agreed.

Justin walked towards Unit Twelve and told him of the plan, which Unit thirty-six then executed, powering on the M.T.T.. The Light-hawk lifted off the ground and flew towards the screen, vanishing. Justin and Unit Twelve then did the same. The portal led them all about thirty feet away from Justin's family cornfield. The group exited the Light-hawk, and gathered around Justin again.

"Gang, we all know what we have to do," Justin said.

Justin turned around and begun to walk towards his parent's house. "Stay here, I'll get my parents, Chris, Unit twelve come with me" As Justin walked to the house, the group talked amongst themselves as Justin entered through the kitchen door.

Justin saw his mom was standing in front of the choirs console working programing the robots to perform cleaning around the house while unavoidably keeping a close eye on the clock, knowing that two days would be up tomorrow morning. As Justin walked through the back door into the kitchen, his mother looked up, ran towards him, and gave him a big hug.

"Oh you guys had me so worried. Where is Chris?" Justin's mother said almost teary eyed.

"I am over here," Chris blurted out as he ran toward her, giving her an equally big hug.

Their mother happened to glance around the room. She noticed a rather odd metal figure standing outside the back door.

"Justin, what is that following you?" Justin's mom said, almost afraid to ask.

"Oh, mom, that's Unit Twelve from the place where we were stranded. He helped us. He is from an alien ship stuck in the middle of the Earth. We have agreed to help him," Justin said, as he began to lead his mom outside to his new large friend.

"Mom, this is Unit Twelve. Unit Twelve this in my mom,"

The two exchanged greetings. Justin grabbed his mother by the arm and tapped the bracelet and was instantly transported back to the Manix IV where Justin and his mom were greeted by the Unit thirty-six, and Unit forty-two.

"Wow!" Justin's mom stared in awe of the surroundings.

Justin explained how the ship came to be in the planet's center, and even told her of his past - future self in cyro.

"I am pretty sure your father will want to see this," Justin's mom said trying to utter the words.

Justin walked towards the M.T.T. and typed in his desired location. He showed his mom that walking through the screen sent you there.

"That is incredible," his mother commented.

Justin and his mother both reappeared in the den. Justin's mom then turned back to the table with the holo COMM and contacted his father, telling him his sons were home. She then promptly began to contact the other parents of Justin's friends, telling them that they had all returned safely and to please gather at her home immediately. The only parents she was unable to contact was Rachel's parents, which she couldn't find.

An hour later, all the parents had arrived at the Haysting house, including both Justin and Nicole's fathers.

The was enough seating in the sunken den, many sat on the carpeted ledge, while others found the couch or chairs brought in from the kitchen.

Everyone was exchanging stories and their views. Laughing was heard. The robots were holding trays with drinks on them, and all had gone out and met Unit Twelve. Most went to the Manix IV to see for themselves the odd spectacle, they were all struck with the awe of the immense size of everything from Unit twelve to the bridge of the Manix IV, and only one or two had seen the Cryo storage only by way of the M.T.T.

As the last of the families had returned to the Haysting home, Justin invited Eric's father and Eric to sit in one of the chairs brought in from the kitchen. "Please everyone, have a seat, Shelly, Tyson, and I will explain a few things." Justin seamed nervous, for he only addressed his peers in school, and not a group like this.

Justin took three chairs, and placed near the back of the den by the walls with the poles, and flagged Shelly and Tyson to come sit in the chairs. The two made their ways through the small audiences and took their seats next to Justin.

Seeing Justin like this, Steven grinned, this was the Justin he missed, this is the Justin with a fire in his belly, and with a sense of wonder and adventure, hoping his son would be able follow this through.

The three huddled together for a moment whispering.

"Tyson, speak first, address the issue about the remains of the Canero robots trapped in the Earth, Shelly, you address the importance's of what's at stake, and I will address the rest." Justin said, the other two nodded their heads in agreement.

Tyson spoke first. "As you undoubtedly are aware, we have encountered obviously quite a problem for both for the humans and the Canero robots, who have shown a desire to have a machine that belongs to them returned. I am more than happy to oblige their request. Also, Shelly and Justin have news to share with you about Planet Wells. Unit Twelve and the other robots gave us a scanning device that would allow us to find the time machine otherwise known to the Canero race as the Matter Transport Transmitter, or the M.T.T., but there is more than just a time machine on that planet. There is a power generator, and a matter phasing device that will free the remains of the trapped ship, in!

side! The! Earth! We believe that if we return the time machine and the rest of the equipment to the machines, the Canero race would be free of their prison, and surely be able to return home."

Shelly nodded, agreeing, then stood up. "I think that we should not delay, though we should act with caution, because this is technology that has been thought of, dreamt of, but just out of reach by man since the dawn of time, and even the Gillenium Council, what they wouldn't give to steal this technology. Thankfully the Canero are a peaceful race," Shelly stated, and then sat back down next to Justin.

Justin then stood, walked two paces, then looked at his father, who continues to smile, Justin smiled back. "Four nights ago, G.O.D. or the Ground Organic Development group unsuccessfully attempted to restore the Earth, they said that the planet was too cold, from the core to the atmosphere, but they couldn't figure why it was so cold, now we have an answer. The Canero ship, the one that everyone took a tour of, I hope you were warm enough." The group laughed. "But with all seriousness, the Manix IV was an exploratory ship, until the Gillenium Council decided to relentlessly hunt down the Canero race, one of the features of the Manix IV is or was its ability to dive into stars to see if they could be powerful enough to sustain life for the new home world of the Canero, one of the stars, and maybe I mistaken" Justin paused again to look at unit twelve, Unit twelve who was listening in through the open outside door from the kitchen.

"Sadly no Justin, we were trapped into your planet before we had a chance."

Justin nodded his head. "Okay, but they had to other stars, but this act of star diving required tons of coolant, when the ship got embedded into our planet, the coolant slowly leaked into our soil, and water tables, cooling our planet. Unit Twelve also informs me that this coolant is incredibly toxic, Unit twelve tells me that they would have a way to clean up the coolant."

"Justin, the coolant is a super liquid CO2, that expanse, the rate that the Earth is going it will be less than another ten years the planet will be completely frozen, but my race has a way of collecting the coolant, and neutralizing the remaining, and from the makeup of your planet, the remaining coolant that's neutralized will become a fertilizer"

"OK, Thanks Unit twelve, well here is where it gets tricky. We have our mission. Now all we need is a plan," Justin said.

Justin's friends and family members were sitting in the Haysting's den they were chatting to each other about how to take action.

"Hey, didn't Justin say he had a plan a few hours ago?" Josh said, slapping Eric softly in the chest as they both laughed.

"What happened to our great and fearless leader?" Tyson shouted with a smile as Justin interrupted.

"I am fearless? No, I am human, and I feel fear, and I felt a lot of it a few hours ago when I saw my nearly lifeless body in a cyro tank. I do not want that to be my future, and I am glad that none of you others were there beside me. Although that is my future, and the age of my body is unknown, that event could happen tomorrow, next week, or next year, or if I am really careful, not at all, but my body is still there none the less, so I could either run, hide, let someone else get hurt for actions that I am supposed to take, knowing they would get hurt, or even die, or do I fight for what's right? Knowing my choices has a price? If it's peace, and freedom and a chance to return back to Earth, than I am willing to pay any price."

CHAPTER FOURTEEN

178 LIGHT-YEARS AWAY

In the deep reaches of space, some 178 light-years away a metallic figure with a reptilian face, a tall, thin bluish pale figure, and another tall red skinned female figure whose beauty radiant off of her skin, were talking in an expandable circular chamber with rows of seats and a stage with a large screen that hovered behind them, in the center was an ever growing spike pit.

Sir Yid, the metallic figure, His expressionless faceplate over his armor was of a lizard like appearance, it's gray and black plates silently moved as it raised its hand and pointed his finger at the thin blue being, it's red rings around its mouth and eyes had a fearful look. "You have failed me. There will not be a next time."

"No, I ordered the Hassar to only follow that human ship, not attack it," Lord Nac Wer pleaded as the white and grey spots flared along his neck and arms.

"Hassar only do as they're told. You must have ordered an attack. Your orders were to observe, and we would act according to council rule, you failed. You will be discarded and replaced," Sir Yid said, picking up Lord Nac Wer by the throat.

"Stop! Killing him will not solve our problem," Trishnar Lina shouted at Sir Yid, grabbing his arm.

Sir Yid flung her arm sideways, knocking Trishnar to the ground.

"I will deal with you later," Sir Yid said glaring at Trishnar.

He then focused back on Lord Nac Wer. "You failed. You're punishment is death."

Sir Yid picked up Lord Nac Wer again by the throat and flung him off the giant stage where below the floor was lined with spikes, impaling him.

"That was a needless death. What do you think you are doing? The Council decides his punishment, not you," Trishnar stated as she picked herself up from of the warm council ground.

"I am the Council, and my decision is final!" Sir Yid said with vehemence to Trishnar.

"So you are defending the humans now, is that it?" Trishnar said harshly.

Sir Yid lifted his metal fist towards Trishnar, "I am all for killing humans, but there were three humans with priceless implants on that starship, gathering invaluable information. If they were killed, then we would have had to abduct more of those gross creatures, and we would have had to start all over again. Besides, those ones we got from the Delta 451 have done our bidding well," Sir Yid tried to explain.

"I understand. What have you learned from these humans?" Trishnar asked.

"I have. Planet Wells has been a primary source of their resources for many years. It is believed that an Earth organization is trying to restore their home planet, without success. With the failure of attempt after attempt, many humans believe that pollutions from their technologies caused the destruction of their environment. Forcing Cut backs on emissions, but that just made everyone miserable, however. They called it 'going green' some sort of environmental movement, but that same pollution helped create a suitable environment on Mars! These Earthlings were fools, and greed drove them to corruption. The greediest of these humans are called politicians, who take bribes, and taxed the commonwealth to death. They even went to the point of rationing healthcare, banking on the idea that people would die before being treated, saving them money. It's pretty evil. I wish I came up with that! I have to take pity on this race. Wiping them out would be a mercy killing," Sir Yid explained.

"I agree. Sorry I said that you had defended the humans. I think I would defend the humans too, especially because the few humans we have taken as slaves are working out great. Turning them into Hassar was easy enough, especially that one we keep around called Hassar Noon, a free will slave, so willing to betray his own race. What a weak-minded species. Does he really think we will reward, but his own death?" Trishnar chuckled, knowing that even with Hassar Noon's loyalty, his only reward would be his own race's doom.

They laughed until a visitor entered the great hall. A tiny figure ran towards the two.

"Sir Tal Con Yid, and Trishnar Lina. I bring news. One of our subspace beacons reports that the humans have means of finding the time machine and believe it's located on the rouge planet, the one the humans refer to as Planet Wells," the small figure said.

"So do the humans mean to use it for themselves, or return it to the Canero?" the metallic figure asked.

"Sir, we believe their plans are to return the lost equipment to the Canero race," the smaller figure said.

"Too bad. It would have made the humans a little bit more powerful. They would have been a challenge, if they had that equipment," Sir Yid said looking sharply at the small figure, which was a Hassar robot, still very small even by Gillinum standards.

"Who is in charge of the recovery party for the Planet Wells time machine retrieval?" asked Tal Con Yid, whose metal body clanked as he folded his top set of arms across his chest.

"A boy called Justin. Sources tell us that John's friend Steve had several children. The oldest is Justin Haysting, and the leader of the group," the Hassar stated.

"Where are they now?" Sir Yid asked.

"The party is organized on Mars, nearly 178 light-years away," the Hassar replied.

"Bring me Hassar Noon. I will need an escort," Trishnar Lina said.

"Right away," the Hassar said as he turned and vanished.

Moments later, a human-sized cyborg Hassar appeared, but even by Gillinum standards the human figure was still very small, seeing that the smallest Gillenium stood over sixteen feet tall.

"You called, Trishnar Lina?" Hassar Noon asked as he kneeled before her.

"Yes, I did. I need 30 units. I am going to make an offer to a little boy that he cannot refuse," Trishnar responded.

"What do you have in mind, Trishnar?" Tal Con Yid asked.

"I am going to have a little talk with this Justin human," Trishnar said, lightly rubbing her fingers across Tal Con Yid's metal chest, and across his face.

"Few men can resist me," she continued, rubbing her back up against his metal chest, then turning around and looking straight into Sir Yid's metal facemask.

"Trishnar, do I need to remind you that my body is in stasis, and my mind has been uploaded into this body armor, and during this time I have no urges of the flesh? Your feminine wiles have no effect on me whatsoever," Tal Con stated.

"But they may work on the boy," Sir Tal Con Yid said, giving her permission to leave.

Trishnar Lina exited the great hall and exited the council building, and made her way to a transport center. There Trishnar entered a room for preparation for her travel to Mars. She stepped into a chamber that shrunk her down to nine feet tall. She left the center to meet Hassar Noon at the shipyard where a golden orb held the ready Hassar escorts. The orb was lifted into a ship suited for smaller beings. The tiny craft lifted off the ground and vanished into the greenish sky.

Many did not relies was that John Parson, Nicole Parson's father, who was married to Laura Parson before her passing from the Martian Syndrome. Before getting a job with the Planet Mining Corporation repairing robots, he worked as an engineer for the military on the Earth's defenses station, Delta 451 under the command of Commander George Swallow.

CHAPTER FIFTEEN

WHO INVITED YOU

Three weeks had passed; John and Steven had contacted the government at the Red House. The president Keystone understood and weighted the ability and resources to the task, and today was the day that a ship, and skeleton crew would be made availability, with exoskeletons that can withstand the high gravity of planet Wells.

Justin and his friends had met several time, and on this day Justin asked his friends, and their families to once again reassemble at the Haysting home.

Shelly was talking to the crowed about their plan of action when one of the house robots approached Justin.

"Excuse me sir, there is a woman here to see you," it said.

Justin walked towards the door, stepped out and spotted a very beautiful woman. Justin had never seen such beauty, or a woman so tall. Justin's neck began to hurt. He cupped it with his hand. The woman knelt beside him.

"Justin, I presume," the woman asked.

He nodded painfully.

"I don't bite," the woman said with a delightful smile.

Justin fought an urge to laugh but smiled instead.

"Wh....wh...Who are you?" Justin asked nervously.

"I am Trishnar. I have an offer to make to you about a piece of equipment that you might be able to find on Planet Wells."

"Planet Wells, right. You want the three pieces," Justin murmured, mesmerized.

"Three, but... Yes Justin. I came to offer you an exchange. Your means of finding these pieces, and I will offer you power," Trishnar stated, as seductively as she could.

Shelly looked around, looking for Justin.

"Has anyone seen Justin?" she asked.

A servant robot approached her.

"Yes, he is outside talking to a woman," the robot said.

"Justin, what are you doing out here?" Shelly asked, pointing to the woman, who now turned her attention to Shelly.

"What do you want?" Shelly demanded.

"This is between Justin and me," Trishnar said, irritated with Shelly's interruption.

"Well whatever you say to him, you can say to me," Shelly said.

Trishnar tapped a button on her belt and five Hassar dropped down from the craft above around the three.

"You're from the Gillenium Council!" Shelly shouted.

Shelly ran toward Justin, and touched him.

"Justin! Hassar!" Shelly screamed.

Justin did not respond.

"Justin! Hassar... Hassar... Hassar!" Shelly screamed frantically.

Shelly grabbed Justin's arm and began to pull him.

"Hassar, kill them," Trishnar commanded, turning around walked back to the small lift that brought her to the planet's surface to ascend back to the craft that brought her there.

Shelly stepped closer to Justin and slapped him across the face.

"What, Shelly? What's going on?" Justin said, coming out of the trance that Trishnar had put him in.

A Hassar dug all four claws into Justin's back, and then slashed his neck. Another came between the two and slashed him in the chest and arms.

Shelly brought the palm of her hand upwards hit what one could safely assume was the Hassars chin, dislocating the head, flinging the body of the machine back a ways from Justin. Justin's near lifeless body fell over backwards, landing on the first Hassar, behind him breaking its arm, though part of it was still lodge in Justin's back.

"No, no, no..." Shelly shouted as she crouched down towards Justin, grabbing onto him, she thought about using the M.T.T. to get back to the Manix IV, but realized that she must have lost her bracelet in the fight, looking at Justin's wrist she saw that Justin was wearing the bracelet, although it was damaged by the attack. Shelly quickly tapped it, sending Justin and herself, with the Hassar that Justin landed on to the Canero ship. The other two Hassar stood for a moment confused, looking all around to see where the three disappeared to until one of the Hassar spotted the bracelet, quickly picking it off the ground managed to store it in a built in compartment in its body cavity, the other Hassar ordered it to run and hide so it would be safe with its find. The Hassar with the bracelet ran until it reached the edge of the corn field, then proceeded to cautiously maneuver inside until it was completely out of sight, even the Hassar thought it was lost, and decided to lay low until nightfall.

CHAPTER SIXTEEN

LIFE RUSH SECOND

As the three materialized everyone on the bridge of the ship looked over to the screen where the three appeared. The Hassar jumped at Shelly from behind Justin, and she kicked it. An orb robot spun a beam of webbing that trapped the Hassar robot. Shelly noticed that there were living beings aboard the ship at this time, and figured that the damaged transport bracelet must have sent them through time.

Seeing the nearest Canero machine, she thought, "If only I could make them understand!"

"Nav, ree, can, nax, ri, tive nac tox, nic, liz, ip wa, lare wick," the figure said.

"I know, I know," she muttered as she left Justin's side, and ran to the nearest unit, grabbed his arm, and pointed it towards her head.

"Please let me know when you can understand me.... Please let me know when you can understand me....Please let me know when you can understand me....Please let me know when you can understand me...." Shelly kept murmuring.

"I can understand you. What is going on here?" the unit asked.

"No time to explain. You have to help him. I hope he isn't dead...." Shelly said frantically.

"I don't know, but we will try to treat him," the Canero said to her.

"Yes, please," Shelly said through her tears.

Unit forty-two's arms stretched out to support Justin's weight, and Unit thirty-six scooped up Justin. Depositing Justin into Unit forty-two's arms, Unit Twelve led the way to the lift followed by some of the living crew. The lift opened as if brand new, Shelly emotionally entangled failed to notice that as soon as the doors closed that they were now on the level of the cryo chambers, re-opening the crowd quickly exited, as the units left, Shelly and the Canero crew followed. The door opened and the three units left entering a room next to the cryo room, where they brought Justin to be treated.

Shelly turned to the Canero. "I am Shelly. I am from the planet Mars. I am from the race known as humans. My friend is Justin Haysting."

"Well then, I am Nockack. I am of the race called Canero..." the Canero crew started to state.

"Well nice to meet you. What about Justin?" Shelly asked.

"Come. We will attend to the situation," Nackack stated as he led Shelly down the hall.

Nackack placed his hand on the wall. The panels opened up and the two entered into the room that had a bench and a window, allowing them to view the three machines and several arms from the ceiling that were operating, trying to save Justin's life.

A small screen lowered from the ceiling. Nackack looked at it carefully as drapes closed around the window. Several hours passed, Shelly paced and prayed her eyes full of tears. Her attention was drawn to the window as the window drapes drew open. Nackack lifted his head from his screen he was studying.

"We have repaired most of the damage; however the spine and other key organs are beyond our repair knowledge. We will have to place him in cryo storage until we have the knowledge. We can however transplant his mind into a holodroid. It will think like Justin, look like Justin, and you will not notice a difference between the two," Nackack stated.

"A holographic duplication of Justin?" Shelly asked.

"It is just until we can get the proper information to save his body," Nackack said.

"Do it," Shelly said disappointedly.

A few machines brought in an endoskeleton that looked like a metal skeleton, but with flat panels with black dots, and many tubes and cylinders that controlled the movement. The holo-endoskeleton that was way too large to be human. Shelly looked at it, and gave a frightful look, as she shook her head from side to side. "It's ok Human Shelly; we will adjust the size to fit your human Justin." After five minutes the endoskeleton was now more of a fitting size, but shelly was surprised, for she never saw the units enter the room with the holodroid, it just appeared, and vanished, returning human sized. Shelly shrugged this off to being delirious from sadness or some other technology that had, that was lost in the accident on Earth.

While the other machines lowered an arm from the ceiling with several thin wires that wrapped around Justin's head. Unit thirty-six lowered another arm with a multi-coloured band of light that slowly ran across his body from the bottom of his feet to the top of head. The endoskeleton sat up. The machine began to emit a light, and then slowly another Justin was standing where once a plain endoskeleton had been. The three other machines then lifted the tray where the real Justin was lying, and moved the body to the next room where more arms were preparing a place for Justin to stay until a cure could be found. There a cylinder was lowered from the ceiling and Justin's body was placed inside. A lid was put on top, and then filled with fluid. The cylinder then rose back to the place where it was first found when Unit Twelve showed it to the group the day before when the Light-hawk was trapped aboard. The three machines returned to the room where Justin's clone was standing.

"Computer: start human subject Justin's memory installation," Unit thirty-six commanded.

"Huh? Where am I? Unit thirty-six, what am I doing aboard the Manix IV?" Justin asked puzzled.

"You were badly damaged. We attempted to repair your body, but we had to put your body in cryo, and place your memory in a holodroid," Unit thirty-six said.

"Holodroid? I am a holodroid? But I...But I...But I…" Justin shuttered.

"Computer: shut down holodroid," Unit thirty-six said.

The body then went lifeless.

"Nackack, the memory is not ready. We will have to return the mind to a time before they entered the ship. It will take a few minutes," Unit thirty-six informed Nackack.

"OK, thank you Unit thirty-six. Well, I guess I could show you around before you go, are there any questions?" Nackack said to Shelly.

"Nackack, how are you here? I thought the crew of the Manix IV was wiped out?" Shelly asked.

Nackack raised his hand.

"Any future knowledge must stay in the future. I have no intention of disrupting the time line. I guess in the future you find yourself here. It is unfortunate that I am not here to greet you. Please walk with me." Nackack raised his other arm to the wall, and the metal panels opened up allowing them to pass through.

Nackack then stepped forward, raising his other arm to show the direction they would be walking. The carpet in the hallway they were walking down was a dull grayish white, the same color as the metal panels on the wall. There were many windows revealing rooms around them and allowing them to view the many other Canero working, repairing, and studying.

"What are they doing?" Shelly asked.

"We are scientists. We study a wide range of fields and find as much as we can, but it just leads to more questions. Of course then it starts all over again. It's really quite silly, but every piece has a purpose in the universe. Life has a meaning, and there is a means to answer questions, but it's finding out why the answers are the right answers, and which are the right questions, and so on and so forth," Nackack said lightheartedly but seriously as well.

"What are you studying now?" Shelly asked.

"A little known sector of space right now. A planet is being formed here. Let's return to the bridge," Nackack said.

"Alright," Shelly agreed.

An hour passed. The ship was in close proximity to what is to become the Earth.

"Right now, only primitive animals live on this planet," Nackack said pulling pictures of creatures.

"Dinosaurs!" Shelly blurted out.

"Dinosaurs? What are those?" Nackack asked.

"They were believed to have existed on my home planet, Earth, billions of years ago. Dinosaur means 'thunder lizard'," Shelly answered back.

"Well we are still in the same area of where your signal was sent, but yes, it is over 40 billion years into the future, so this must be the Earth you spoke of," Nackack speculated looking deep into the image.

The frozen Hassar shook, as it broke its bonds, and then was able to move its arm, then a leg, freeing itself, both arms, moving, slashing, struck the webbing. It broke free, and lunged towards the ground. The others on the bridge moved from their panels and consoles in fear of injury from the tiny machine. Just as a large oncoming meteoroid was spotted close to the ship collusion was emanate.

"Sir, we're going to have to move...." one of the Canero said, just as the Hassar assassin struck.

The Hassar then leapt on the person at the control, and slashed him.

"Nackack, the Justin holodroid is ready," Unit thirty-six called over the ship's P.A. system.

"Bring him up immediately. Those two others should leave now. It is no longer safe for the humans," Nackack said, trying to maintain control.

The lift doors opened. Unit thirty-six was escorting Justin. Justin ran to Shelly and hugged her tightly. Nackack, now badly injured by the Hassar, made his way to the M.T.T. and programmed a return passage for the two. They vanished, and Nackack died shortly afterwards. Moments later the ship was struck by the meteoroid. A large piece of the ship broke off, and the ship was pulled into the planet.

CHAPTER SEVENTEEN

BAD OUTCOME

Justin grabbed one of the falling Hassar and threw him against the Light-hawk. The little droid broke apart and fell to the ground.

"Run." Justin said, The group made their way to the open door of the garage ushered by Justin, pushed by the blast from the Hassar as the unit exploded, scorching the side of the Light-Hawk.

Justin and Shelly bolted back into the garage, and accessed the Light-Hawk remotely through the house network.

"I'll start the Light-hawk. Everyone hold on to something, this is going to be bumpy," Justin said.

The Light-hawks primary thrust engaged and the four remaining Hassar were sucked into the engine. A fire was started on the exhaust ports of the Hawk, flames shooting out of the side, catching the shelves and sighting in hot dancing plums of superheated inferno spreading to the Haysting house.

Justin quickly located the ship that Trishnar traveled in and set the Light-hawk on a collision course. He hopped out and the ship lifted off the ground still on fire. Justin ran to a drawer nearby and took out a pair of binoculars. He could see the two ships, but the Light-hawk exploded before hitting the alien transport. Still, it was enough to knock the ship out of its orbit, and as it began to descend it started to break up. It crash-landed, creating a crater, a ball of rubble and no survivors.

"Good work, Justin!" Josh said, patting him on the back. "What about the sensory equipment though?"

"I guess we will have to get another one from Unit Twelve, but everyone, good work! Let's see how everyone else is doing," Justin said.

"I say Justin is our leader!" Tyson shouted.

"No, I am not leader material, but I am responsible, they got us into this mess, we will get us out." Justin said leading the group around the house threw the red dusty walk way to the front of the house.

The six entered the house from the front door, the bathroom was locked tight and a trembling voice came from inside near the floor.

"Is it safe to come out?" Nicole asked, peeking her head out the door.

Inside the bathroom Nicole, Rachael, and Lucy plus many of the parents were hiding from the attacking Hassar.

"Yeah, we took care of them," Justin said with a smile walking towards Nicole.

The door slid up from the bottom reviling that many frightened folks still shaking. Tara peeked out and started walking throughout the house.

"Curtis, Curtis, it's safe to come out." Tara called still searching for her son.

Justin and Nicole joined in the search, passing over Eric's unconscious half covered body.

"Has anyone seen Curtis?" Tara said looking around frantically.

Eric slowly awoke, his half naked body still lying on the ground. There was a quick flicker and layer of tan slacks materialized around his lower half, as well as a collared shirt with buttons down the middle on his upper half. He sat up, feeling the cold presence of a fluid on his hands.

"Blood! Blood!" Eric screamed.

CHAPTER EIGHTEEN

MORE REASONS TO ACT

He saw that Justin's younger brother was lying lifeless on the ground, the hand of a Hassar still lodged in the body. Eric raced over to try to wake the small child.

"Wake wake wake...please...ok ok ok...be be....wake wake... please!" Eric shouted, shaking the boy.

But Curtis did not respond. The little boy did not survive the Hassar attack. The others gathered around. Tara frantically cut through the crowd and kneeled at the side of her son, throwing the Hassar hand off to the side. She picked up her son, and began to wail, squeezing the lifeless body, staining her clothing with his blood, her face twisted in "That was a narrow escape," the now Holo Justin said turning to Shelly.

"No kidding!" Shelly responded.

"Whoa, he's an android, but I can hardly tell. It's as if he never got hurt in the first place," Shelly thought to herself.

Shelly and Justin landed back on Mars in their time, and in the same place that they were last, but looking around they noticed that there was now smoke rising from the hangar. Both Shelly and Justin looked at each other.

"The Light-hawk!" they both shouted, as they helped pull each other off the ground and rushed to the now blazing hangar.

As the two turned the corner, they saw Steve and John in exoskeletons fighting several Hassar. Tyson was ripping one apart with a sickle, while Josh was attempting to smash another with the remains of one of the robot servants.

"What's going on?" Shelly asked.

"They're looking for the sensory equipment," Tyson said using the sickle to trip another Hassar.

"Where is Eric?" Justin asked.

"He passed out after seeing the Hassar barge into the house," Josh said throwing down the remains.

"Are there any more?" Shelly asked.

The four heard clanks above them, and saw a claw cut through the ceiling of the hangar, making a hole through which six more Hassar dropped down.

"Does that answer your question?" Tyson responded.

grief. Sobbing, she lay in the fetal position on the floor wrapped around her son. Justin, Chris, Sam, and Steve, approached, their faces red, tears staining their cheeks as they began to mourn the loss of their family member.

One of the robot servants alerted the emergency response team, which landed shortly after receiving the call. They rushed into the house. Steve put his arms on his wife's back, and turned to the team.

"Please give my wife and me a moment please," Steve said.

Tara slowly lifted up, unwrapping her arms from Curtis' lifeless body. She turned and put her head on Steve's shoulder and hugged him. Two of the emergency response crewmembers held their arms out as a holo-cloth sheet extended from their hands, covering the little boy's body. A hover stretcher slid underneath and projected a black shell over the top. They then moved out towards the small craft the team had arrived in. Tara, Steve, Justin, Chris and Sam followed it outside. One of the crewmembers found the Hassar hand. The crewmember projected a bag, and slipped it over the hand, continuing outside. Outside the other members of the emergency response team treated the other victims. Many only had minor cuts and bruises, although nothing would treat their emotional scars. The Haysting family hugged, and then Tara and Steve followed the medics that treated the wounds to their vehicle, a squat boxy shaped carrier, but bright white and yellow vessel with flickering lights on every corner of the craft. The back of the craft lifted allowing the stretcher to slid and secure it into position, two of the medics walked to the front of the vessel, as the other climbed through the rear open hatch. Steven and Tara followed getting inside the emergency response craft. The other members of the team finished up, one by one loading onto the ship.

The ship was an orbital ambulance with a crew of six. The tiny craft could drop to anywhere on the planet to render assistance, and on board was enough room for two extra passengers and one person to lie on a stretcher.

The orbital ambulance doors closed, and everyone outside returned to the Haysting home. Justin and Chris stayed outside to watch as their mom and dad leave with the body of the other brother. Shelly felt worse than the others, because what seemed like moments ago she was able to save Justin, but she wasn't in time to save his brother, and she blamed herself.

Nicole wrapped her arms around Justin, crying with him. Justin slowly got up and asked Nicole, Chris, Tyson, Shelly, Josh, and Eric to join him in the den.

"This is clearly a message, one that was meant to scare us into giving the sensor equipment to the Hassar," Justin said, looking towards Eric who was the last to have the equipment.

CHAPTER NINETEEN

UNIT'S FORTY-TWO GIFT

"Have... it... not... I," Eric said.

"Oh, please tell me you didn't give it to the Gillenium Council!" Justin said, concerned.

"Hid... no... I...didn't...it...I...did," Eric said, with a sad smile.

"You hid it? Good thinking. Now, no one except the Hassar and the Gillenium Council is to blame for the death of Curtis, my brother. Eric, get the sensor," Justin said with authority. "We need to take action, now."

"A plan? So you have a plan? Does that make you our leader?" Tyson asked.

"No, I told you I have a responsibility, nothing more. But we have work to do," Justin commented back.

The group gathered together once again. Nicole asked her father to join the group.

"Mr. Parson, I need you to secure another vehicle. I am also going to need several exoskeletons. Also I need to see if there are any of the mining robots on Planet Wells we could devote to our cause," Justin said.

"Justin, you don't need to do this," John stated.

"I know, but I need to do this for Curtis," Justin responded.

In a matter of hours three ships had landed by the Haysting's small house. Several large metallic bodies walked off the smaller transports; afterwards the transport lifted off the ground again and in a flash, was gone.

"Justin Haysting, if you could please sign here," an officer said as he walked towards Justin holding a light pen and a holographic form displayed in front of him.

"What this for?" Justin asked.

"A ship, these exoskeletons, robot mining support, and a few officers we could spare as a crew," the officer replied.

"Wow," Justin gaped, signing with the light pen.

The vessel was known as the Felix One, a military war ship, streamlined design, with updated sensors, computers, and other systems that were way more advanced than the Solid Luck. The Felix One was faster than the Light-hawk, Justin like the colour of the ship, almost a dark red, with yellow lines that outlined the energy output of the main engine, the sections of the line brightly pulsed as the energy passed through.

Shelly would feel more comfortable with a professionally trained crew, and maybe for once maybe operations would go according to plan, but the government could only spare what was in the reserves, it's not that they weren't grateful by any means, but expected a bigger deal to be made, and understood that Mars forces were spread pretty thin.

"Justin?" Nicole asked.

"Yes?" Justin answered back.

"Unit thirty-six and forty-two want to see you. Here is my wrist bracelet," Nicole said handing him the bracelet.

"Oh, thanks, I guess I'll go see what they want." As Justin slipped the bracelet on, and quickly vanished.

"thirty-six, forty-two, you wanted to see me?" Justin asked as he passed through the M.T.T.

Unit forty-two approached Justin, raised his hand up, and the once broken orb zipped to forty-two's hand and landed.

"I and the rest of the drones here abroad the Manix IV wanted to give you a present to help you on your journey, and your mission to return us to our home world," Unit forty-two said as it handed Justin the small orb.

"Thank you forty-two. Why is thirty-six being so quiet?" Justin asked.

"Thirty-six used parts from himself to fix the small robot, in hopes that he would be able to help with your quest," Unit forty-two answered back.

"He didn't have to do that," Justin said.

"We're machines, and Unit Twelve is the most capable machine to help you. We're old and broken, nothing more than parts," Unit forty-two said.

Justin held out his hand and the small orb zipped towards Justin's hand and landed in his hand.

"Justin, you can tell him to follow, or pick up small objects like tools. He can also access the computers for you," forty-two stated.

"Alright, I'll give it a try," Justin said.

"Orb, follow me," Justin said, as he walked toward the computer console.

The orb followed, and Justin smiled.

"Orb, access the M.T.T. Send me back to Mars, at the coordinates I came from," Justin told the orb.

The tiny orb split in half, and the different sections spun in opposite directions. Then the great screen flickered to life and showed the cornfield from whence Justin had materialized.

"Follow me," Justin said as he walked towards the screen, and turned back to Unit thirty-six and forty-two.

"Thank you," he said, walking through the screen to the cornfield on the other side.

CHAPTER TWENTY

PERMISSION TO BOARD THE FELIX ONE

Justin continued inside to the newly landed ship the Felix One. The group was already inside, all except Lucy and Rachel.

A tall officer in a green uniform greeted Justin as he approached the entry ramp.

"Permission for me and my orb to board," Justin said to the greeting officer.

"Permission granted. Welcome abroad," the officer said to Justin.

The officer proceeded to produce a holodisplay, showing it to Justin.

"What's this?" Justin asked.

"Standard uniform, and equipment that can be produced by holo-cloth." The office replayed.

"Oh, okay" Justin pushed his thumb through the crewman's display downloading the equipment.

With the new information Justin changed into the crew's uniform, looking at the new outfit. "Neat" He exclaimed.

"Who is in charge?" Justin asked the officer.

"Captain Daniels is the commanding officer, but I hear that you are the one in charge of the mission," the officer responded.

"Really, I am Justin Haysting. You can call me Justin," Justin introduced himself.

"I am Officer Scott Thomson," the officer replied.

"Can you show me to the bridge, please?" Justin asked the officer.

"If you will follow me," the officer replied as he sealed the heavy hatchway large hydraulic pistons closed tightly.

"This way" The officer said pointing down a dimly corridor, gray interior, with support beams that jutted out from the walls.

"What is the crew compilation onboard the Felix One?" Justin asked.

"There are twenty crewmen onboard, and your group of eight," Officer Thomson answered.

"Eight? Did Nicole come aboard?" Justin asked puzzled.

"I don't know all their names, but they are waiting for you on the bridge," Officer Thomson responded.

Moments later both Justin and the escorting officer reached the bridge. The bridge didn't appear to have chairs, yet a few officers were sitting, sitting in midair. Some of the officers were siting high up, at other controls, but Justin couldn't make out what that was that kept them afloat. As for the controls, most of the displays were holographic projection, projecting in blue and cherry colours around the bridge.

"Justin, please have a seat." Officer Thomson offered,

"Where, I don't see any chairs.

"The holo-cloth your wearing has an integrated disk seating system, don't worry it will support you."

"Th… disk… what?" Justin asked.

"Disk seating, you see that disk on the right side of your paints just below your pocket?"

Justin looked down, and noticed it. "Yes, I see it"

"Good, there is a smaller disk on your left side, and by your knees."

Justin took a quick moment to look, and also noticed that there were similar disks on his elbows and a line that went to the bottom of his wrist. “Okay, now what?” Justin asked.

“Just sit down” The officer explained.

Justin unsure about sitting on a magnetic field, carefully he lowered his back end, bending his knees, sure enough he felt as if the disks were there supporting his weight.

Justin looked up at Officer Thomson. “See, you’ll get the hang of it, also you can kick yourself around like if you were in a regular chair too”

With a look of wonder, Justin gave a gentle push; sure enough Justin began to glide across the bridge.

“Now to stop from moving, simply touch the center of the disk on the right.”

Justin touched the center, and sure enough he was held tight. “Then to move again do I touch the disk again?”

“Yes, you’re a quick one; also if you want to change heights of the chair, slide your finger up or down to adjust your height on the bridge.”

Justin reached for the disk, running his finger up the center of the disk, took him up a little ways where his feet could no longer reach the floor. “Okay. This is awesome, but how do I stand up?”

“Oh, just stand up, and the disk system will disengage”

Justin tried, even the tips of his shoes were too high to touch the ground, and then he remembered he could swipe down on the disk bringing him closer to the floor. Once closer to the floor he was able to stand.

“Also Justin, if you slide your finger around the disk downwards you’ll recline your chair, and upwards to bring it back you, it controls the metal disks along your back, there are six of them that create the back of the chair.”

“Amazing.” Justin commented.

A loud tone played threw the bridge boatswain call followed by an announcement. "All hands prepare for lift off," an officer announced over a speaker system.

Josh ducked when he saw the small orb that Justin brought aboard the Felix One.

"Is that... Thing... dang... dangerous?" Josh asked remembering the impact on the Hawk.

"No, the other drones aboard the Manix IV used their own parts to fix this little guy, and they said that it would help us. Besides, he's harmless," Justin said with a smile.

Nicole noticed Justin from across the bridge, and ran towards him and embraced him in a big hug.

"Nicole, I thought you were going to stay behind?" Justin asked.

"I don't want to miss this. Besides, I can handle myself, even when it comes to battling the Hassar," Nicole said smiling.

"Nicole, there are going to be a lot worse things thrown at us than just the Hassar," Justin said putting his arm around Nicole.

Tyson pointed to a door.

"Yeah, we saw how you handled yourself. Well, next time we're attacked, there's the bathroom," he said laughing.

Justin frowned at Tyson.

"Tyson, that was some pretty quick thinking, getting the parents to safety," Justin said, complementing Nicole's good judgment.

A door from the other side of the bridge opened up, and a tall figure approached Justin. The man why was in a dress uniform, with two arms that extended up over his shoulders, and joints with the rest of the arm hung down with grippers that rested on top of his shoulders. The man extended one of his lower arms, and outstretched a hand towards Justin.

"I am Captain Daniels. You must be Justin. I have heard so much about you. Nicole went on and on about you. You are a lucky young man," Captain Daniels stated.

"I am pleased to meet you. What's with the..." Justin said, taking the extended hand.

"Extra arms? Before I came into command I was an engineer, and in those days most of the equipment was hardwired into our bodies, and connected straight into our brains. The extra arms housed a variety of tools as well. Nowadays the communication of man and machine is simplified with the use of the nanites we take for granted," Captain Daniels explained, giving a good strong squeeze to Justin with his handshake.

Justin pulled his hand back, and projected the image of bandages wrapping themselves around his hand.

"It's not that bad. I didn't use full force," Captain Daniels laughed at Justin.

Justin stepped back towards his friends.

"Four arms, he has four arms," Justin kept muttering to himself almost in shock.

"I'll see if the nurse can give you an extra set for yourself if you like," Captain Daniels said as he put one of his extra hands on Justin's shoulder.

"Umm, umm, No... No thanks," Justin muttered.

The captain laughed. Justin mustered up the strength to address the captain.

"Captain, may my friends and I use your briefing room?" Justin asked.

"This is your mission. I don't see why not. Lieutenant Hid, open inertial COMM," Captain Daniels stated.

"Channel open, Captain," Lieutenant Hid responded.

"This is the Captain speaking. All of Justin's group and senior staff please report to the briefing room for orders. Captain Daniels out," Captain Daniels stated, escorting Justin to the meeting room with Nicole and Josh following behind.

CHAPTER TWENTY-ONE

ADVANCING THE PLAN

As Captain Daniels and Justin entered the meeting room, he saw Eric, Tyson, Shelly, Chris, Nicole, and Josh.

"Ladies, and gentlemen, please be seated. Go ahead Justin," Captain Daniels spoke.

As Justin walked toward the semi-circle room, he saw the table was made of bright blue and purple plasma, cool to the touch. The chairs that surrounded the table were made of a highly polished metal, with no legs. Instead they floated about two feet above the ground on a cushion of plasma. As Justin stood there, he whispered to the orb that had been following him. The orb zoomed off. The light in the room dimmed, and Planet Wells was projected on the silver wall behind him.

"The Canero lost more than just a part of their ship here, and I lost more than just my family. I fear that the Gillenium Council will stop at nothing. Today our families were attacked because they wanted to get to us. The death of my brother, the loss of the Light-hawk, are all because we have the possibility of acquiring what the Gillenium has been after for so long. Eric, go to main engineering and hook up the sensor. Josh, I need you to go to navigations. Tyson, and Shelly I need you to set up the exoskeletons," Justin said with determination.

"What about me?" Nicole asked.

"What about you?" Justin asked back.

"What do you want me to do?" Nicole said, feeling left out.

"Well… Go to the communication center."

"Yes?" Nicole asked.

Add our COMM channels to their frequencies. The rest of you, let's meet back here in an hour," Justin ordered.

The group went their separate ways, each with a task in mind. Justin walked with Captain Daniels.

"So let me get this straight. How are we going to land on Planet Wells when this ship is not suited for the high gravity?" the captain asked.

"Well you're right, but we're not going to land. Shelly, Tyson, and Josh are going to suit up for the high gravity, travel to the Canero ship, and use the coordinates from the sensors. We will then use the M.T.T. to go to Wells, and your crew will direct us on the planet surface," Justin formulated.

"Nice plan. You'll make a great captain one day. Are you sure you don't need a few extra arms?" the captain joked.

Two hours later the group met back in the conference room to report on their progress.

"Thank you for joining us. Eric, were you able to hook up the special sensor to the ship's system?" Justin asked.

"Sir, finished... charm.. works...like...the...works," Eric spoke in a broken fashion.

"Good, good. Thank you, Eric. Josh, what have you found out?" Justin asked.

"Justin, it will be another ten days before we reach Wells. We already have charts of Planet Wells on file here, and we will have detail of the terrain before we reach there," Josh spoke.

"Thank you, Josh," Justin acknowledged. "Shelly and Tyson, status of the exoskeletons?"

"All eight of the suits are in perfect working order," Tyson stated.

"It's going to take a bit to fully operate one. I recommend that since we're due to arrive in little over a week, we should train in them," Shelly suggested.

"Excellent. Thank you Tyson. Shelly, I agree. I'll meet you in the cargo hold. Nicole, what about communication systems?" Justin asked as Tyson and Shelly stood up and exited out to the cargo hold.

"The exoskeletons have a COMM system, and we will be to communicate while you're on Planet Wells, but you'll be out of communication range when you go to the Manix IV," Nicole reported.

"Great. Josh, keep studying the planet. Eric, I want you to scan for temporal dilation fields. We don't want a repeat of what happened to the "Deus Ex Machina.", and use the coordinates from the sensors. We will then use the M.T.T. to go to Wells, and your crew will direct us on the planet surface," Justin formulated.

Thought to be lost, the Deus Ex Machina, a scout ship sent to search for planets rich in resources, the vessel with a crew of ten, first explored the outer rim of the sol solar system, spotting a large planet with large quantities of rare earth minerals, and many compounds not found on earth. As the Deus Ex Machina got closer and closer to Planet Wells, they were hailed by another vessel, a vessel thirty years more advanced than their current technologies. They found out that the small scout ship had slipped through time. The planet was later named Wells after the author H.G. Wells after one of his popular books, *The Time Machine.*

"Nice plan. You'll make a great captain one day. Are you sure you don't need a few extra arms?" the captain joked.

The group took extra care for their first mission, and took time doing what they could in the short span of time they were allotted, but after two hours the group met back in the conference room to report on their progress.

"Thank you for joining us. Eric, were you able to hook up the special sensor to the ship's system?" Justin asked.

"Sir, finished... charm.. works...like...the...works," Eric spoke in a broken fashion.

"Good, good. Thank you, Eric. Josh, what have you found out?" Justin asked.

"Justin, it will be another ten days before we reach Wells. We already have charts of Planet Wells on file here, and we will have detail of the terrain before we reach there," Josh spoke.

"Thank you, Josh," Justin acknowledged. "Shelly and Tyson, status of the exoskeletons?"

"All eight of the suits are in perfect working order," Tyson stated.

"It's going to take a bit to fully operate one. I recommend that since we're due to arrive in little over a week, we should train in them," Shelly suggested.

"Excellent. Thank you Tyson. Shelly, I agree. I'll meet you in the cargo hold. Nicole, what about communication systems?" Justin asked as Tyson and Shelly stood up and exited out to the cargo hold.

"The exoskeletons have a COMM system, and we will be to communicate while you're on Planet Wells, but you'll be out of communication range when you go to the Manix IV," Nicole reported.

"Great. Josh, keep studying the planet. Eric, I want you to scan for temporal dilation fields. We don't want a repeat of what happened to the "Deus Ex Machina."

Thought to be lost, the Deus Ex Machina, a scout ship sent to search for planets rich in resources, the vessel with a crew of ten, first explored the outer rim of the sol solar system, spotting a large planet with large quantities of rare earth minerals, and many compounds not found on earth. As the Deus Ex Machina got closer and closer to Planet Wells, they were hailed by another vessel, a vessel thirty years more advanced than their current technologies. They found out that the small scout ship had slipped through time. The planet was later named Wells after the author H.G. Wells after one of his popular books, *The Time Machine*.

CHAPTER TWENTY-TWO

DECKS AND SUITS

An hour later Justin, Shelly, and Tyson were suited. Harnesses materialized around their chests, with straps that attached around their thighs, over their shoulders, and onto their upper arms. Helmets with visors cradled their heads and breathing masks with hoses hung loosely from their helmet straps. All were wearing jumpsuits. Shelly often wore a deep purple one, but today she toned it down to an off-white suit with purple trim. Justin, who had a habit of wearing black, felt like a light color for today's exercise and choose a light gray suit with black and blue trim. Tyson, whose favorite color was red, overindulged with bright red. Shelly and Justin had to squint just to look at him.

Four of the Felix One's crew were there. They wore dull grey jumpsuits, grey being the standard issue color. They prepared to enter their suits to train for the high gravity. The exoskeletons were roughly three meters high. The yellowish paint that coated the suits appeared scraped off in areas showing that they once had a great deal of use. The housing area folded open, exposing the cockpit. There were no windows, except for a few portholes with thick glass, now replaced by plasma screens. There was a sensor package placed on the front of the suit, now with updated technology, and a view screen inside that allowed the user to see.

Justin gave the suit a verbal command to kneel, and the suit complied. The left leg stepped back, and the knee bent towards Justin.

"Cockpit open," Justin commanded.

The suit followed through. Justin fixed the breathing mask over his mouth, turned 180 degrees and stepped backwards into the suit.

"Lock and pressurize," Justin commanded, as he quickly hooked the holes to the life-support system.

Tyson, Shelly, and the other crewmembers did the same. Planet Wells' powerful gravity was enough to crush flesh, but the suit had enough strength to move freely in its gravity. The pressurized system allowed one to survive on the planet's surface.

As the seven began to move about, lift equipment, tool and weapons, run, and jump, the inexperienced pilots fell, bumped into each other, or just plain fell over. The crew of the Felix One had more training with the suits, and had training drills with large two-handed weapons, and suit-mounted shield emitters.

"Wow, I am glad they're on our side," Justin said.

"No kidding!" Shelly exclaimed.

Tyson went to the weapons rack, and picked a large assault rifle. He marched over to the first crewmember in line for him to inspect his weapon.

"Very good. Do you wish to join our exercise, Tyson?" the leading crewman asked.

"Yes sir. I would, sir!" Tyson shouted back.

"OK, this isn't basic training, cadet, just a simple 'yes' or 'no' would do. Oh by the way I am Scott Thomson, but you can call me Scott, or Scotty," Scott said extending the suit's hand out.

Tyson approached and tried to shake it, missing the first few times. Finally Scott grabbed Tyson's hand after another failed attempt, and shook it.

"OK Tyson, get in line and try to keep up," Scott said.

Tyson tried to follow the movements of the crew. At first he started simple, holding the gun in front of him. Then he held it to aim through. Shelly and Justin watched and laughed as Tyson began to do jumping jacks, then run in place, falling several times.

"Josh, you need suit training. Get down here," Justin said to a COMM system.

"Are you serious?" Josh asked.

"How are you going to be our guide on the planet's surface if you are up on the ship?" Justin said.

"I don't know. I am very tempted to try the suit, but I don't know. Besides I'll be able to guide you from the ship," Josh said reassuring.

"OK, suit yourself," Justin laughed.

The three continued to train for seven of the days during travel to Planet Wells. After Justin had finished he hopped through a shower.

"Shelly, Tyson. Please meet me in the conference room as soon as you can," Justin said over the COMM system.

Justin exited his sleeping quarters: a small six meters by six meters room with four bunks, and an adjacent shower and bathroom attached. The floor was lined with several footlockers to store personal effects. The room had two desks at the end of each row of bunks. Justin continued down the hall.

"Justin, what's going on?" Shelly asked.

"Wait for Tyson. I need to talk to you both," Justin said.

The two entered the meeting room. Captain Daniels and Tyson were there.

"What's going on, mister?" Captain Daniels asked harshly.

"Well Captain, I wanted to meet up with the Canero machines, and inform them of what's going on, and get some more information," Justin said nervously, trying to explain.

"I understand. When you were planning to tell me?" the captain asked.

"As soon as I knew who was going," Justin responded.

"OK, that's fine. This may be your mission, but this is still my ship. You're more than welcome to use my meeting room, but it would be nice to know when you want to use it," Captain Daniels said.

"Yes Captain, sir," Justin responded.

"Good. Now, who is going with Justin, and who is staying here?" the captain asked.

"I'll go," Tyson said raising his hand.

"Me too," Shelly said swatting at Tyson's raised hand.

"Ow, hey," Tyson said to Shelly with a smile.

"OK," Justin said pressing his bracelet and vanishing.

Shelly followed.

"Hey, wait for me!" Tyson shouted, as he picked up the rear.

CHAPTER TWENTY-THREE

THE M.T.T. AND DAGGER IN THE BACK

Unit forty-two stood near the M.T.T. as Justin materialized, pushed forward by Shelly, and then pushed by Tyson, knocking over Justin.

"Be careful, Justin. We don't want two of you down in cryo," Unit forty-two said.

"Thanks Unit forty-two. Hi, how are you?" Justin asked.

"Hey Unit forty-two," Tyson said.

"Evening," Shelly said.

"What a nice surprise! What brings you humans here?" Unit 42 asked.

"Well, we're here because we're getting pretty close to Planet Wells. The planet with your technology on it, and we have come to request your help getting there," Justin started.

"Sure, by all means, but the gravity is so high on that planet, that we are useless on that planet," Unit forty-two responded.

"I am sorry to hear that. We could have used your help. However, we have powered suit that can be used to move freely in the high gravity, we didn't want you to be startled when we came through in these suits. Also I'll have the little orb program the coordinates in," Justin explained.

"Well I thank you for thinking of us, and can I help you in anyway?" Unit forty-two asked.

"Yes actually, how can we shut down the phase cloak system?" Shelly asked.

"You will not be able to, unless you disable the generator, but by doing that, you will not be able to use the M.T.T. to get close enough and I'll program your orb with the instructions to shut it down. Then re-engage the generator while touching the phase cloak and you will be phased with it. You be able to manually shut it off, then the M.T.T. will work again," Unit forty-two explained.

"Great, here is the orb," Justin said, plucking the little orb hovering around his shoulder.

Unit forty-two took the orb to the computer panel, and placed it in a slot. The orb began to spin as three arms thrust into the metal. Sparks leapt for a moment, then the arms retracted, and the orb stopped spinning. Unit forty-two pulled the small orb from the console.

"I upgraded it for you," Unit forty-two said.

"Orb upgrade?" Justin asked.

"Why, yes. I placed the same sensory equipment in your orb as in the hand held device you received from us earlier," Unit forty-two said gleefully.

"Wow that should be really helpful!" Justin said.

"Now you three, I must ask you to run along. We're testing if this ship is going to be space-worthy, and I don't think it will be safe for organic humans," Unit forty-two said rushing them out.

"OK, orb, set the coordinates back to the Felix One," Justin ordered the little orb.

The orb once again split open, a small dial started to spin, and the M.T.T. flickered on. Justin, the tiny orb, Josh, and Shelly stepped through.

"OK, they're gone," Unit forty-two said, pushing a button on a display screen.

CHAPTER TWENTY-FOUR

THE DAGGERS TWIST

A door on the side of the bridge opened.

"Good work. You programmed that orb of his with the tracking system?" Trishnar Lina asked.

"I did as you asked. You'll be able to see what the orb sees and know where they are at all times," Unit forty-two said.

"Ha ha ha ha, those little twerps won't know what hit them. I'll strike them when the M.T.T. is down. They won't be able to escape this time," Trishnar Lina said ecstatically, walking to the control panel and typing in her coordinates.

"Hassar, follow me," she said walking towards the M.T.T. screen.

A hundred Hassar followed her through to her ship in orbit on the other side of Planet Wells.

For three days Justin, Shelly, Josh, and five other crewmembers of the Felix One continued training. The war ship Felix One had begun its descent into an elliptical orbit around Planet Wells.

"We have arrived on Planet Wells. Justin's team to the bridge," Captain Daniels said over the COMM.

Shelly and Tyson piloted their suits to the side of the cargo bay so they could exit their suits more easily. They then exited into the hall. Eric was performing some last minute adjustments to the sensors, tuning them so they could pick up minor temporal waves.

He secured the last panel and wiped his brow with his sleeve, then stood up from a crouching position, waved to the other engineers, and walked into the hall. Josh was placing a couple of flags on the giant map of Well's surface, including the mining dig sites, and passable location of where he thought the lost Canero technology would be located. The scanner table where Josh had been working also showed the maintenance craft the robots used to meet the repair ships in orbit, and Josh was using simulations to learn to fly it safely out of the high gravity so that Justin, Shelly, Tyson, and the other crewmen could bring back what the Canero lost. Hearing the command to come to the bridge, Josh saved his work, turned off the screen and exited the Nav room. As each person arrived, all they could do was staring at the front screen showing the Planet Wells, all of them were in awe of the richness, and the transparent of the formidable planet.

"Cool, isn't it?" the captain said.

"That's a planet," Josh said.

"Yep... I mean sure, I was studying the maps, and I just thought that the picture was kind of faded..." Josh said.

"Nope, the whole planetoid is ten percent transparent, giving it this awe-striking appearance," Captain Daniels said, looking around the room. "Hey where is Justin? You'd think he would be here by now."

"Sorry I am late, guys," Justin said as he sprinted through to doors that led to the main hall of the ship.

His eyes were red, and his face was flushed and puffy.

"What happened to you, Justin?" Shelly asked.

"Oh, I am sorry, I was overwhelmed with the loss of my brother," Justin said feeling his eyes tear up.

"it's okay; you will make them pay" Nicole said putting her arms around him.

"Thanks Nicole. Wow, look at that planet," Justin said trying to be strong.

"Yep. Eric, scan for temporal signature. Josh, give us a layout. Tyson, Justin and I will get suited up. Let us know the coordinates to materialize to," Shelly said, knowing that this was the moment of truth.

Justin, Shelly, and Tyson walked down the corridor into the cargo bay. The three suited up, and the other crewmen were all ready to go.

"Justin, I have the coordinates. I am sending them to your orb."

"Thank you. We will contact you as soon as we are on the planet's side," Justin responded.

"OK, guys. This is going to be the most difficult challenge that we will ever face. Out there, an enemy, who is willing to chase mankind halfway around the galaxy because of an object, that object of great power, and that enemy wants to control that object, for with its power, is capable of removing all barriers that distance burden us with. Today we risk our lives to see a better tomorrow, a tomorrow without fear, a tomorrow without needless bloodshed, a tomorrow where we can know that we don't have to continue watching over our backs, because I have a feeling we are walking into a trap, but that's to be expected. Who's with me?" Justin said proudly.

"I am!" the group shouted.

CHAPTER TWENTY-FIVE

NOW OR NEVER

"Great. Let's get that equipment, and let's do this!" Justin shouted.

Tyson touched two of the crewmen in their suits and vanished. Shelly followed with two others.

"Are you ready, Scott?" Justin asked.

"Ready and willing," Scott responded.

Justin extended his arm out to Scott, and they materialized on the Manix IV.

"Justin, Shelly, Tyson, is that you?" Unit forty-two asked.

"Yes Unit forty-two, it is us. This is Scott. Scott, Unit forty-two," Justin said, introducing the two.

"Nice to meet another human," the friendly Unit forty-two extended his greeting.

"Nice to meet you as well," Scott said.

"Justin, do you have a moment? I need to speak to you," Unit forty-two said, grabbing the orb and shutting it off, then pulling Justin away.

"Sure, what's on your mind... processor?" Justin commented.

"A very tall, strange lady visited me, just before you arrived to tell me what to expect when you reached Planet Wells," Unit forty-two tried to explain.

"Oh, a fan," Justin said with a smile, looking back at Shelly. "Hey Shelly, we had a fan stop by to talk to us."

"A fan?" Shelly started to walk towards the two.

"Justin, was it Trishnar? Trishnar came here?" Shelly asked Unit forty-two nervously.

"Yes, a Trishnar, had visited..." Unit forty-two said as Justin interrupted.

"Trishnar? Who is this Trishnar?" Justin asked.

"She asked to speak with you, outside of your house after we returned to Mars. She wanted the scanning equipment, and when I interrupted her she sent the Hassar after us, killing your brother," Shelly continued to explain.

"I don't remember. Come to think of it, I can't remember what happened to me after returning to the Manix IV with my mom," Justin said, very worried.

"Why can't I remember, and why was it when I returned home I was with you, Shelly? And the Hassar was attacking? Why can't I remember, Shelly? Why?" Justin asked, frantically trying to think and remember.

"If I can't remember, but it happened, then the only way I wouldn't remember is if I was unconscious, and if I was unconscious, then I must have been injured, and if I was injured then, what does that make me now? It makes me not me," he said, questioning himself.

"Unit forty-two, tell me what happened," Justin demanded of Unit forty-two.

"Not now Justin," Shelly said harshly. "We'll come back to it, I promise. Let's go."

"I am sorry Unit forty-two. Tell me when we make it back. Anyways, so this Trishnar woman comes here and..." Justin asked.

"The orb we gave you, she made us put a location and tracking device in it, and has been following you. Where she is now, we don't know because almost all the systems on this ship are non-functional and no way of finding her, she is probably at the site now," Unit forty-two concluded.

"Oh no, she must have received the information Josh loaded into the orb," Justin said thinking out loud.

"Yes, hurry. She was already in orbit around Planet Wells when she came here," Unit forty-two said.

"OK. Does she know that my body is in cryo here?" Justin asked.

"No, I never told her. You are safe," Unit forty-two said, comforting him.

"OK, I'll deal with it later. Let's go, everyone!" Justin shouted, getting the orb from forty-two, and turning it back on, then sending the orb to set the M.T.T. for the Planet Wells.

"Justin, you can't take that orb..." Shelly tried to explain.

"We need to. It's the only way to turn the generator off, and be able to return part of the Caneros ship to their people," Justin said in defense.

Tyson exited first with two of the crewmen. All three fell to the surface, and struggled to get up. Shelly and the two crewmen went through, landing on top for the crewmen Tyson brought through.

Justin thought it would be best to enter from the far side of the screen seeing how often time people got stacked on top of each other when choosing to travel through the M.T.T.

CHAPTER TWENTY-SIX

TOO LITTLE TO LATE

"That damn machine. I knew it would betray me. Well, I'll be ready. Seems like there are eight of them to my hundred Hassar," Thrishnar giggled as her own powered suit kicked up Planet Well's soil. She was followed by a trail of Hassar to the site of the Canero 's lost parts.

Justin reached a hand to Tyson helping him up. Tyson then grabbed the two crewmen's shoulders and lifted them up. Scott helped Shelly up. After Shelly was on her feet, Scott and Shelly helped the other two crewmen up. Tyson and the other crewmen then kneeled down to pick up their weapons.

"Justin to Felix One, do you copy?" Justin said through the COMM in his suit.

"We copy you loud and clear," Nicole said.

"Good. We are about sixty meters away from your pinpoint of the Camero technology. We got a warning from Unit forty-two. He told us that a Thrishnar was on the planet, and that she has Hassar, lots of Hassar, and that this Thrishnar may already have a ship in orbit," Justin replied back.

"OK, we will keep on the lookout. Good news Justin, the military has sent three extra ships, with extra suits," Nicole said happily.

"That's great, when will they be here?" Justin asked.

"In about a day," Nicole replied.

"Good, that will give us enough time to reach the mining robots, and the maintenance craft and find a place to safely stay," Justin said.

"OK, I'll patch you through to Josh and he'll guide you," Nicole said.

"Hello Justin," Josh said.

"Hey Josh, I need directions to the mining robots, and the maintenance ship. I'm all ears," Justin said back.

"Justin, what about the orb?" Shelly asked Justin.

"What, this guy here?" Justin said with a smile holding the orb up.

Shelly looked at the orb, "What, I don't get it?"

"Unit forty-two switched the orbs," Justin tried to explain.

"Come in, Justin. This is Josh,"

"Go ahead Josh. What's going on?"

"Justin, the maintenance ship is about six hundred meters south of you. I'll forward you a topographical map for you via your suit's computer," Josh COMMed the group.

"Great. I'm pulling it up now." With a quick look at the map, Justin noticed a small dark circle near a large crater.

"Looks like someone has an ambush set up," Justin said over the COMM.

Shelly glanced over the map.

"Thrishnar! What do we do, Justin?" Shelly asked.

"Well let's fight robots with robots," Justin said.

The eight sprinted towards the maintenance ship. Reaching the ship they saw the name on the side. It read "Fur Ball" in Filinease and consisted of ten large cranes that stood out like large strands of hair.

"OK, Josh. Knock for me and see if anyone is home," Justin joked.

"OK, Justin... Hey wait a second," Josh said to Justin.

"There is someone on board."

"Hassar?" Justin asked.

"Thrishnar?" Shelly asked.

"Someone from the Gillenium Council!" Scott shouted.

"No, he's friendly," Josh answered.

"Oh yeah! I remember now, My dad told me about him. Jinxinton, but everyone calls him Jinx. He's a felionsapion," Justin said smiling.

"Felia-what?" Shelly asked.

"They're a race of cat-like beings," Scott added.

"We were on patrol of a border near their home world," Justin said.

CHAPTER TWENTY-SEVEN

CAPTURED

"Who is it, what do you want?" Jinx hissed.

"Hello Jinx. I am Justin Haysting. My father is Steve Haysting," Justin said, introducing himself.

"So? You want a medal? Wait, did you say Haysting? Then you're Justin. Yes, your father spoke very highly of you! Please come," Jinx said invitingly.

The eight entered and began to remove their exo-suits.

"Justin, are you there?" Nicole said over the COMM.

"I am. What's going on?" Justin asked.

"Good news and bad. The Dayless and the Rogers arrived in orbit," Nicole replied.

"That's great," Justin said with glee. "What's the bad news?"

"Two Gillenium ships have arrived. We're taking fire," Nicole said.

"No way, you guys be safe," Justin said, running towards the maintenance crafts center console.

"Jinx, two Gillenium Council ships have arrived in orbit, and are attacking our ships. Where is your radar display?" Justin said frantically.

"What matter would it make?" Jinx replied calmly.

"There is a war going on overhead, don't you want to watch?" Justin said, getting angrier.

"I thought we had an ambush down here. Let's concentrate on that shall we?" Jinx said walking towards Justin.

Jinx passed by the captain chair of the Fur Ball, and palmed a small pullout pistol and continued walking towards Justin.

"Everyone gather round," Shelly said joining Justin at the radar.

Justin linked the suit's computer to the radar and began pulling up the topographical charts of the planet to see the best way to approach Trishnar and her small army of Hassar. The rest of the soldiers from the Felix One gathered close behind.

Justin straitened himself up from the computer console, and turned to Jinx. "How did you know there was an ambush set up… you… didn't… Even know we were coming," Justin said cautiously.

"Very good, Justin," Jinx said cutting through the small crowd to stand near Justin.

"I did know. Someone beat you here, and her offer was better than what the humans were offering."

"But we didn't make you an offer."

Jinx look at Justin in the face. "Exactly." And laughed, then grabbing Justin by the shoulder, Jinx spun him around and pushed the nose end of the pullout pistol into Justin's back. Clapping was heard from the other side of the room as Trishnar ducked through the doorway. Behind her, the room filled with Hassar.

"Very good! Very good indeed Mr. Jinx, and Justin, last time I saw you, a Hassar had split you in half. I thought you would be dead, but here I find you, without a single scratch. I watched you right after the attack, and you and your girlfriend over here disappeared. 'How did you get M.T.T. technologies?' I thought to myself. Your little race isn't advanced enough. Then I found you of your bracelets someone dropped, and tapped its control, which led me to the ship in your home world."

The gears in Justin's head started turning. "If this is true than there would be two of me in cryo, but Unit forty-two joked he didn't want two of me there. One of you must be lying to me."

Justin turned to look at Shelly.

Shelly started to cry. "I thought that the only way you would survive is if I took you to the Canero ship, only to find us on the ship before it crashed into the Earth."

"So you mean that I am not me?" Justin asked.

"No, no. Stop it! Stop it!" Shelly said through her tears.

"What am I?" Justin demanded.

"That's what I would like to know," Trishnar said under her breath, bored.

"I can't. I can't tell you, Justin." The memory flashed through Shelly's mind of the holodroids of Justin discovering what he was, screaming out as the Canero doctors and scientists shut him off and erased his memory to try again.

"OK, this is cute and all, but I don't care about your personal lives. All I want is the lost tech here on the planet. I'll kill you later. OK, Jinx. You have somewhere you can put them until Sir Tal Con Yid arrives?"

"Sure, in back… Huh?" Jinx said, noticing a message on the screen of Justin's arm.

"What's this? A message?" Jinx tapped the controls.

"Justin do you read me?" Nicole said over the COMM.

Jinx put his hand over Justin's mouth.

"Jus-jus-Justin is not here at the moment, what's going on?"

"We have taken too much damage. We're going down..." the COMM said before falling silent.

"I guess the call was dropped," Jinx said, as he and Trishnar laughed.

They ushered Justin and his group into the back holding area to wait for Sir Tal Con Yid to arrive…

www.ingramcontent.com/pod-product-compliance
Lightning Source LLC
Chambersburg PA
CBHW070359200726
48294CB00003B/993

* 9 7 8 1 9 6 1 2 5 0 2 9 1 *